CARNIVAL CURVES

I0885887

CARNIVAL CURVES

STACEY ROBINSON

JAMES LORIMER & COMPANY LTD., PUBLISHERS
TORONTO

James Lorimer & Company Ltd., Publishers acknowledges funding support from the Ontario Arts Council (OAC), an agency of the Government of Ontario. We acknowledge the support of the Canada Council for the Arts. This project has been made possible in part by the Government of Canada and with the support of Ontario Creates.

Cover design: Tyler Cleroux
Cover image: Shutterstock

Library and Archives Canada Cataloguing in Publication
Title: Carnival curves / Stacey Robinson.
Names: Robinson, Stacey Marie, 1978- author.
Identifiers: Canadiana (print) 20250188562 | Canadiana (ebook) 20250195429 | ISBN 9781459420014 (hardcover) | ISBN 9781459420007 (softcover) | ISBN 9781459420021 (EPUB)
Subjects: LCGFT: Novels.
Classification: LCC PS8635.O264 C37 2025 | DDC jC813/.6—dc23

Published by:
James Lorimer & Company Ltd., Publishers
117 Peter Street, Suite 304
Toronto, ON, Canada
M5V 0M3
www.lorimer.ca

Distributed in the US by:
Lerner Publisher Services
241 1st Ave. N.
Minneapolis, MN, USA
55401
www.lernerbooks.com

Printed and bound in Canada.

Dedicated to the brilliant artists and visionaries — on stage and behind the scenes — who pour their hearts into Caribbean Carnival year-round. A tribute to the generations of Caribbean descendants and our international peers who find joy, healing, and liberation in this powerful cultural experience. Thank you for keeping the beauty, spirit, and history of mas alive!

CHAPTER ONE

Carnival Season

"Karla! Baby girl!" my aunt squealed, standing up from her seat to greet Mom and I with a hug at the entrance to the bright Scarborough warehouse where costume production and other parade preparations were taking place for the city's upcoming Caribbean carnival.

There were groups moving tables, chairs and pieces of lumber. Drilling echoed in the background, along with a large flat-screen monitor playing a Trinidadian news station. The audio rang through stacks of speakers set up in each corner.

"A-ki-lah," Mom said to her little sis, imitating the newsreader's island accent that was clearly not her own. "Ready for another season, gyal?"

"Court-ney! Of course I'm ready!" Auntie Akilah responded,

hugging us to her sides. "I've missed you both so much!"

Mom was excited to have Auntie Akilah — or Akie, as I called her — back home in Toronto, where they were both born. They were besties and laughed together on the phone every single night, just like me and my girl Nneka.

I took a quick selfie with them and WhatsApp-ed it to my cousin Jamar, Akie's son.

Karla: Reunited!

There were boxes filled with long pink ostrich feathers opened around us on the workstation, a wooden table. Auntie Akilah sat on her stool, gesturing to the four charts laid out neatly before her on teal stationery.

"You're always so organized," Mom said, shaking her head in awe. Akie was all ready for the season, though she'd just returned to Canada the night before, after living in Fort Lauderdale for years.

Akie moved to the United States after high school on a track scholarship and graduated from Florida State University with a sports therapy degree. She always made college life — and life in general — look so cool. She was one of the reasons why I was so excited for my own journey at Toronto Metropolitan University in the fall.

My cousin responded to my text with a few smiley faces.

Jamar: Ma Dukes got you beading carnival bras already? haaaaa

Born and raised in the American south, Jamar lived with his father and was never a fan of the Canadian cold. He was finishing up his first year at Florida Memorial, a Historically Black University, studying biology.

Karla: Yup and I'm here for it!

Jamar: I miss her already. I'll be in The Six soon tho. Hail up Auntie Courtney and Uncle Patrick for me.

Karla: kk

Akie was a physiotherapist, Uncle Garfield was an orthotist and Jamar was now taking his ideas to TikTok with these wacky but creative knee and joint videos for athletes and dancers. They were all a ton of fun, and he was building a little following online.

"Mom, Jamar said to hail you up!"

"Aw, tell him I said hey and I miss him." Ever since Akie and Uncle Garfield divorced a few years back, Mom had been begging her sis to return home to be close to family.

Plus, we were a quiet bunch and could use some excitement.

"Ugh, I wish we could all be in the same place at the same time for once. Now Gran and Pops are missing out," I said, exaggerating a frown. My grandparents had returned to Ocho Rios, Jamaica, a few months back to the retirement home they had been slowly building for almost ten years. My free-spirited older brother Dorian moved to the island to live with them. With our family members gone, Toronto seemed a bit emptier. Akie was back just in time!

"Mama and Daddy are aright," Akie said. "Don't worry, hun, we'll all be together for Christmas."

"True, true . . ." I said. We had a family trip to Jamaica planned for the holidays.

"But, Courtney . . . since you're here at the mas camp, I have to ask, are you gonna join me on de road this year?" Akie said. We had to laugh because we all knew. Mom wanted no part of the crowded carnival parade.

"As if," Mom said, rolling her eyes. "I didn't do it in high school when I had the energy for it, and I certainly won't do it now."

Mom's idea of a good time was sitting on her special couch with her Kobo, reading the latest celebrity tell-all and drinking a glass of wine. Dad was a TFC fan and would watch their games and any other football matches. They were both homebodies and always had been.

I was falling into their habits and looking for something to shake me up a bit and bring me out of my comfort zone. "We both know that's not going to happen," I reminded Akie with a smile. "But now that I'm eighteen . . ."

"*You?*" Mom said. "I never heard you express interest in carnival before, babes. Do you even like the music?"

"I'm just sayin'." I shrugged and played with one of the feathers. "Why not? I can get down with soca music!"

"Absolutely!" Akie agreed. "And you will look stunning in my costume!"

"These materials are so pretty," I said. Wide-eyed, I looked at the shimmery pink fabric with its iridescent glow, the boxes of jewels and the rows of wire spread across the other tables around the warehouse. I wondered if I could get away with wearing a t-shirt over the costume! I had been wearing a t-shirt over my bathing suit ever since I was twelve, when a boy at the beach commented that Jamar and I had the same body. Mortified, I waited patiently for my feminine shape to blossom. At eighteen, I was still waiting.

Beside each workstation stood a shiny black plastic mannequin, ready to be dressed in a carnival costume. Next to it was a message board on a stand listing the costume's details. On Akie's table, her pink and teal sign read:

LIBERATION MAS PRESENTS

"SWEET WINE"

FOR TORONTO CARNIVAL

SECTION: Rosé Rendezvous

SECTION LEADER: Akilah Johnson

ULTRA FRONTLINE: $1400 female

FRONTLINE: $975 female | $750 male

MIDLINE: $675 female

BACKLINE: $400 female / $350 male

CONTACT: Akilah@LiberationMas.com

"Fourteen . . . hundred . . . dollars?" Mom said. She shook her head and let out a deep breath, wide-eyed. "These are works of art, but I can't believe so many people spend this coin on costumes each year! I thought these were about three hundred. Even two."

She looked around to see if other costumes were similarly priced, but most of the costume makers were still just setting up their workstations.

"Girl, the costumes haven't been two hundred dollars since we were in high school doing the soca butterfly," Akie told us. Mom laughed out loud. "Miami Carnival is the same. It's expensive but worth it. Cost of materials. Labour."

"I don't know why I thought it was so much cheaper than that," Mom said, running her fingers across the fabric.

"People invest in their passion . . . and the experience, you know?" Akie said, shaking her shoulders in an exaggerated shimmy. "They get the costume, a nice goodie bag, refreshments all day, make new friends, hear good DJs . . . plenty dancing. It's worth it!"

"Akilah, girl, you don't need to sell me on this. My money is staying right in my bank account so me and Patrick can go build a lil' house next to Mama and Daddy when we retire," Mom said. We both knew Mom was serious — they would love nothing more than to sit in the shade on a veranda in Jamaica and read all day long, sipping on freshly squeezed orange juice. "Well, I think Miss Karla will have much more fun working here with you this summer than her previous gigs," she added.

Akie had invited me to assist with her carnival costume production. Every year, on the Saturday before the first Monday of August — our civic holiday in Ontario — the city of Toronto was electrified by the sounds, foods, costumes and spirit of Caribbean culture.

I'd never attended the parade, but I saw a lot of it on TV news and Akie's Instagram photos and video clips as she carnival-hopped over the years. She built costumes in Florida but would travel to participate in other carnivals in St. Lucia, Barbados, and even the West Indian Day parade in Brooklyn, New York, over Labour Day weekend.

Everything I knew about carnival, I knew because of her social media. Akie was a carnival addict (it was literally her hashtag), and it only made sense to give it a try. My bestie Nneka and I always watched her social media videos and photos and admired how magnetic Akie's vibe was. Always smiling, laughing, dancing and celebrating her culture, she visited carnivals everywhere and shared the experiences with us through her images.

"Your designs have gone international!" Mom said, giving her sis a high five. Akie was amazing. She managed to do her rehab work and still build up her costume business on the side. "I can help putting together those goodie bags for the masqueraders — that'll be fun."

"Thanks, Court. I'll email you the list of everything and transfer the funds later in the week. You can take your time to source things out and set up shop at home," Akie told her. I knew she was giddy to have us all work on this project together before starting her new full-time job in the fall.

CHAPTER TWO
Mas Camp

"This is going to be fun!" I said, clapping. I'd actually be making more money with Akie than at my regular summer job with the recreation team at the community centre. I was ready to try something new.

"How's school going, babe?" Akie asked. She was packing up for the day, and we were going to go out for ice cream after she gave me a tour.

"It's good. The university acceptances are coming out soon, so we really just have to maintain our grades," I said. I was counting down until the end of the semester when I could enjoy my summer before commuting downtown to TMU.

"I'm so proud of you," she said, squeezing me again. "Come! Let me show you guys around."

Mom and I followed as she walked us to the back of the warehouse and spread her arms; we could see the entire room buzzing.

"The mas camp!" my mom said knowingly. "If I had a dollar for every time I heard Akilah talk about *the mas camp* back in Florida."

"Meh place!" Akie laughed.

"Yuh place!" Mom added in her faux island accent.

An older lady with beautifully smooth, dark brown skin, a sturdy round frame and inviting eyes walked up to us with an armful of glittery white fabrics. "This yuh family? These must be your sisters, allyuh have the same eyes and nose," she decided with a wide grin.

Akie introduced us to Ms. Ingrid. We smiled and nodded again, unable to shake her fabric-filled hands.

"Welcome to the Liberation Mas camp," Ms. Ingrid said.

Akie explained that Ms. Ingrid was the Liberation Mas band leader, along with her sister, which meant they were the CEOs of their own carnival business. They planned the theme and activities for each season, selected designers to make the costumes and made sure the Liberation team had a comfortable space to work, bond and enjoy the preparations together.

"Have you played mas with us before?" Ms. Ingrid asked, looking at me.

"No, this will be my first time."

"Well, I know you'll have a great experience with us. Liberation is a good community, and a lot of young people have been joining lately." She kissed my cheek before floating away.

Akie introduced us to a few other folks and then showed us the front office, where sketches, parade route maps and costume sample pieces were lying about. Some older men were putting together a display wall of plastic vines, while a young woman with thick, long locs was doing electrical work behind them.

Everyone was so kind — I could swear Mom was even having second thoughts about joining us.

"This our band's chef and his wife," Akie continued, pointing out various areas of the mas camp and introducing us to those in our path. "They own the Caribbean Oasis restaurant at Kennedy and Lawrence." They greeted us like family. "We've all been planning over Zoom for the past few months, so it's awesome to see everyone in person now."

"It's our time of year, gyal," one of the young ladies said to me, bumping me with her hip as she passed with a mannequin head in her hands.

It was already exciting. "Thanks for inviting Nneka to join us," I said to Akie, who was having a hard time finding another local assistant. Nneka usually worked at the hospital with her mom, picking up extra administrative work, but now that high school was ending, she expressed that she wanted to get out more and recruit some cuties to date.

"You girls will have a blast," Mom said. "And Akilah can share all of her carnival wisdom with you!"

"That's why we're here, baby girl," Akie said, gesturing at the people around us in the mas camp. "From Florida, to Yard, to TnT, to Atlanta. And now, from Notting Hill to Toronto . . . it's our duty — and my pleasure — to pass the culture on to you."

CHAPTER THREE

Band Launch

Nneka's older brother Ekene dropped us off outside a banquet hall in an industrial part of north Scarborough with rotating floodlights at each end of the parking lot. We slowly approached the entrance with our printed tickets. Hearing the bass thumping against the walls, we entered the venue timidly. Dry ice escaped from the doors to the main ballroom.

Liberation Mas was hosting their first event of the carnival season: the launch of their masquerade band and the reveal of the season's costumes.

"Girl, super exciting!" Nneka said, pursing her lips. Her deep brown skin was always flawless, with the right amount of foundation and just enough highlight. Her cheekbones popped — her face card never declined, natural or with full glam. An expert makeup artist, Nneka had given herself a sultry look for the night with smoky eyes and a cute black jumpsuit.

"Extremely," I agreed. "Okay. Let's not miss one single detail!"

She nodded her long boho braids to the soca song playing. Her mom did both of our hair, and never missed. My knotless braids were in a low ponytail; I was casual in a new pair of white jeans and a simple blue crop top.

Burgundy lights projected across the auditorium walls like liquid, and there were plastic wine glass structures around the room. "Sweet Wine," the year's theme, glittered across a huge banner. Life-sized cardboard cutouts of costumed masqueraders — men and women dressed in beautiful, bedazzled outfits from previous years — stood in the corners.

"*Eeks!*" Nneka said, squeezing my arm. We walked to the side of the stage and saw our names placed on the backs of chairs. Akie had reserved two spaces for us to experience the show up close.

"I think I'm going to like it here," I said, and Nneka nodded, moving her eyes from one illuminated object to the next.

"Evening, ladies," an athletic hottie said to us both, taking the seat next to Nneka. I recognized him from the TFC. His friend — equally hot — followed behind him, nodded and sat down. We smiled and said hello, shyly. Nneka sat up straighter and kept her smile bright as we continued to look around.

Off to the side of the stage there was a brass band. I wasn't familiar with a lot of soca music, but the sounds were festive and I nodded and moved my shoulders along with the rhythms. Nneka chair-danced along with me while we watched the crowd fill up the venue.

Within an hour it was standing room only. When the lights dropped, so did my stomach. The tuba played a dramatic bassline and a dozen dancers wearing shiny gold bodysuits with low necklines took their positions on stage. The brass band faded and the DJ began to play a familiar calypso oldie I'd heard my Pops play.

Six costumed dancers pranced out to join the gold ladies. They wore sheer black bodysuits with beaded gold accents at the top, nude fishnets and high black stilettos. Their skin glimmered from all angles; their long gold eyelashes were fierce. They bent down at the same time, circling a lady who backflipped and landed smoothly in her heels, launching the routine.

"Eh eh!" Nneka whispered. "This is Olympic-level."

The troupe of ladies grooved with grace to every beat. People cheered and whistled. Someone blew an airhorn, and almost everybody danced along with them.

I was too excited not to clap. Soon, others around us were

clapping too. I let out a cheer, applauding as the routine came to a close.

"Them girls ate down!" Nneka said, squeezing my arm. Touch was definitely her love language, and I knew my arm would be sore by the end of the night. It was Nneka's best and worst habit!

Ms. Ingrid came on stage with a microphone, dressed in a shiny black blouse and elaborate gold skirt. Her short and curly natural hairstyle had small gold jewels in it. "Welcome, welcome! Carnival season is here!" she exclaimed. "Welcome to the launch of Liberation Mas, and our presentation of Sweet Wine for Toronto Carnival!" Applause.

After some more words about their sponsors, her sister Ms. Gladys exclaimed dramatically: "Without further ado, we present to you . . . Sweet Wine!" They walked to the podium at the side of the stage.

The lights went down and a solo steel pan began to play. I felt another pinch on my arm. Nneka couldn't contain herself!

A tall, slender, chocolate-skinned man dressed in a gold loincloth strolled on stage, barefoot and serious. He paused at the end of the runway and surprisingly started to sing. I didn't understand the language, but his deep voice was strong and resonated throughout the room.

"That's an Igbo song," Nneka whispered. Her parents

were Canadian-born, but both sets of her grandparents were from Nigeria. "I thought this was an island people t'ing?" The singer/model continued to croon.

"Owww!" a female voice cheered from the back of the room, followed by catcalls from other women in agreement. The singer looked down modestly and continued to speak in his language.

I looked at Nneka, raising an eyebrow. "What's he saying?"

"Something about community and love and . . ." Nneka paused. "Something about new life and . . . liberation? Ah! Liberation. My Igbo ain't that good," she said, chuckling. When we were younger, she used to take lessons on Saturday mornings with a Nigerian elder who helped her to learn the language. Her parents barely spoke Igbo, and even when talking to family back in Africa they usually communicated in English.

After the poem, the man walked majestically to the back of the stage and paused. To the left and right of him emerged two beautiful, brown-skinned women wearing Akie's costume — I recognized the neon yellow bodysuit, pink and teal feathers and the gold accents.

"Our first costume of the evening is Rosé Rendezvous, designed by Akilah Johnson," Ms. Ingrid said while a soca song began to play.

The women in costume began to dance down the runway

with spotlights on them, feathers fluttering as they took control of the stage. My eyes were fixed on the pretty headpieces with gold and teal gems hanging along the models' hairlines, and the gold choker-style necklaces that matched the straps of their bikini tops, worn over a neon yellow bottom and sparkly gold fishnets.

"If I had a body like that, I would rock that string bikini too!" Nneka said, clapping. "Gorg!"

One woman was wearing a neon yellow and pink bikini with an elaborate, equally colourful feathered backpack and headpiece, in addition to multiple jewels across her arms and legs. She extended each limb to highlight the details.

"This must be the fourteen-hundred-dollar costume," I whispered.

"It's so incredibly pretty!" Nneka gushed while the girl in a simplified version of the same costume walked to our side of the stage, raised her hands, and paused for the photographers, vloggers and bloggers standing in the special media area. She was wearing a barely-there version of the bikini, a combination of jewelled neon yellow strings and tiny patches of pink fabric wrapped and tucked around her body. Her headpiece was simple, a jewelled tiara.

A male model was next, with fitted teal Bermuda shorts on; he was shirtless with a pink and teal belt and matching bands around his calves and upper arms. He had a teal jewelled headband on and surprised us all with a quick backflip before making his way down the stage.

"Whoa," I said, taking a few pics with my phone.

"Wonderfulness!" Nneka agreed, recording a quick video for Snapchat. Akie's costume was just one of eleven that would be featured in the presentation.

The costumes were all beautiful. Akie's pink design was followed by ten others, introduced one by one, each with their own set of models. There was Candied Cherry in red, Bordeaux Bodies in orange, Albarino Vines in yellow, Melon Zinfandel in green, Licorice Moscato in blue, Violet Sauvignon in purple, Naught Pinot Noir in black, Copper Merlot in brown and Sauvignon Blanc in white. Dozens of smartphones lifted in the air, snapping and livestreaming to their personal audiences.

When the final costume, Cranberry Chardonnay — a deep burgundy — took a lap, all of the models from the evening paraded across the stage one last time for more photos and applause. The audience danced along with them and the music continued as feathers swayed and jewels sparkled. Finally, the last set of bum cheeks could be seen shaking off the stage.

CHAPTER FOUR
Nakedness

Nneka and I looked at each other and exhaled deeply. She squeezed my arm. “So fun!” she exclaimed.

“So fun,” I agreed, turning to look around at the crowd.

“And so naked,” she added, widening her eyes. “They are literally Instagram models. No way regular girls can wear these ribbons in public.”

“That’s what I was thinking! All that fabric at the mas camp had us fooled! There’s hardly any fabric at all!” I raised my hand to my face. “But it’s all so pretty!”

“Facts,” Nneka agreed. “But look at dem cuties!” She used her lips to point at the line of young men who just entered the venue, banging enthusiastically on tassa drums. “Ayeee! Knock it!” she cheered along, shaking her shoulders to the

Indo-Caribbean rhythms.

People around us started to mingle and the DJ continued to rock. A few of the models came into the crowd, dancing and smiling with the audience as they gathered around the bar and greeted each other after a long winter break from carnival. Nneka and I bopped as we looked through the photos and video clips on our phones until I felt a tap on my shoulder and saw Akie behind us.

"What did you think?" she asked. She was dressed in a hot-pink one-piece spandex bodysuit and had amazing stage makeup on, highlighting her pretty eyes. Akie was slim and cute. Confident in her body, she could wear anything and look good.

Nneka looked at me quickly, shaking her head. I got her cue, and didn't bring up our concerns.

"Everything looked ah-mazing!" I said.

Two of Akie's costumed dancers lingered closely around her, still shaking their hips and extending their arms to the sounds of the drums. A younger male videographer paused to record Akie as well, kissing her cheek before he continued to walk.

"So, so beautiful," Nneka said. We followed Akie to the bar area where she ordered us two ginger ales and a beer for herself.

"You made all these alone?" I asked.

"I did. I like to make the samples myself just to make sure

everything is exactly how it needs to be," she said. "We'll probably have about a hundred more to do, all being well."

"Do you think we'll be able to handle it?" I asked, looking around. I could see a few familiar television reporters and top vloggers interviewing participants.

"Of course," Akie said, clinking her beer can against our glasses in cheers. We gushed about the designs and dancers for a bit, while the afterparty started around us. "Okay, I promised your moms I'd have you home early and before the liquor started flowing . . . so . . ." She looked down at her phone and opened the Uber app. "Your chariot will be out front in four minutes, and I will see you two on Tuesday, okay?"

"Thanks, Auntie Akilah. This was fun," Nneka said, giving her a quick hug.

"Thank you so much!" I said, joining in.

"Message me when you're both home safe," she reminded us. "Look out for a silver Toyota Corolla, license plate ending in 688."

I nodded, placing the empty glass on a table close by, and started to walk through the crowd with Nneka close beside me. The force field of dancing around us was electric; I knew we'd be up late sharing videos and fantasizing about what the summer months would bring, working with these beautiful materials and vibrant community.

CHAPTER FIVE

Baddies

Going back to school on Monday felt like travelling back in time. Nneka and I didn't have many classes together. I chatted with my lab partners Omar and Isabella in the morning, as we often did while doing the day's assignments, showing them footage from the band launch. Our science teacher was cool like that and didn't mind us on our phones as long as our assignments were completed.

"Baddies. Every one," said Omar, casually taking my phone from me to scroll through the photos and video clips again. "Maybe I should play mas with you guys this year," he teased, raising his hands and wiggling on his stool.

Isabella laughed. "You?" Omar played drums for our school's senior concert band and was always about his music.

"Dancing on the road? I'd see you playing in a band on a truck, maybe."

"What? You don't think I can get down? Rubber waistline?"

"Of course you can, Omar." I nodded, keeping a straight face. "We'd just rather hear you drum."

"My cousin plays with the steelpan band PanTastic. They don't need a drummer, and believe me . . . I asked," he said, picking up our worksheet and opening the cupboards at our station to search for supplies. "Let's get this over with."

My one class with Nneka — English, that afternoon — was quiet as we had reading time and worked independently on our final projects. Our friend Chelsea, who Nneka and I had known since kindergarten, sat beside me, whispering about her ongoing crush on Omar. When Nneka and I asked her to join us for our carnival experience, Chelsea laughed. "I don't have the confidence to wear one of those costumes in public!" Nneka and I exchanged a quick look, knowing that we actually agreed.

After school on Tuesday, Nneka and I asked Ekene to drop us off at the mas camp to start our first day of work. Once we pulled into the parking lot of the small plaza, I could hear the bass of the soca music already.

Ekene usually rolled his eyes when we asked him for a ride. This time, however, his eagerness made sense when we saw all the women lingering outside unpacking costumes and materials.

"Ekene, you come to look woman?" Akie said, reading our minds.

"Hey, Auntie Akilah," he said shyly. "Welcome back to Toronto!" Nneka and I both held back chuckles. "Just trying to make my sister's life easier."

"We both know that's cap," Nneka said.

"Thanks, babe. I'm glad to be home," Akie said, as we prepared to head in. A few now-familiar faces smiled and waved at us.

The room was covered in colours and sparkles in every direction, with beads and lighting illuminating each corner. It was so pretty. At the back of the warehouse there was a sales desk with a receptionist, cash register and costume details on a printed menu.

"Welcome back!" I heard Ms. Ingrid greeting us. She was fixing up the display mannequin at the Candied Cherry workstation beside us, hidden behind a mass of red feathers.

"Thank you!" Nneka and I said in unison, hovering close behind Akie. We sat down at her table and watched as she opened her binder.

"I've made this very official for you so you can track your hours and have some skills to add to your resumes, okay?"

Akie said, handing us the papers while she started to break down the costume options to us, with photos from the band launch as her guide.

"The majority of our orders will come in for the backline costumes," Akie concluded, pointing out the optional pieces. "If they want to order hot shorts instead of the bikini bottoms, that's an option we can add on. If they want to order a tank instead of a bra top, that's also an option. It all depends on their comfort level and what style they prefer."

We both let out sighs of relief, making Akie laugh.

"We were worried!" I expressed, covering my face with my hand. "Those models were dancing around in strings and we were scared!"

"Terrified!" Nneka agreed with a laugh. "Options sound good."

"Don't worry, it will all make more sense as we go along and you see examples," Akie promised us, rubbing my shoulder in comfort. "Keep it all in perspective, okay? There's a business side and a culture side in addition to the parade side. Everyone plays their part!"

Akie then gave us an overview of the key events of the summer. Aside from the scheduled costume production days at the mas camp, we would help her with events, and prepare to bring all hands on deck to the band leaders and other costume creators as they got ready for the Junior King and Queen Showcase, and the Junior Parade in mid-July. The children's version of "Sweet Wine" was called "Sweet Soda" and featured a colourful set of costumes for the kiddies to parade in.

"Remember, the carnival is a competition, so our goal is to make our band look the best . . . and win! That includes helping the others if they need extra hands." Akie handed us each a special pink plastic carrying case. We opened them to see our own set of scissors, measuring tape, pins and a glue gun. "These are your tool kits, and this is your weekly schedule."

Around 7 p.m., a few young men filtered into the mas camp, cool as ever with backpacks on and sharp fits. They passed by each of the workstations, including ours, pausing to respectfully kiss the section leaders on their cheeks before proceeding to the back area where the DJ stand was.

"Who is heeeee?" Nneka whispered to Akie, pointing to a fair-skinned cutie with soft curls wearing a black Raptors hat and black and gold Liberation Mas DJ t-shirt. He had a confident swag and Nneka was already captivated.

CHAPTER SIX
Orientation

"Girl, you are so predictable," I said, laughing. Nneka definitely had a type. "I think the older guy is DJ Jump Start, right?" I remembered seeing his interview on TikTok after the band launch. He was Indo-Caribbean, from Trinidad, and his wife was one of the models, an Afro-Trinidadian woman. They were speaking about how they grew up participating in carnivals back home, and how they were raising their son with the same traditions in Toronto.

"Yep," Akie said, as her phone began to ring. "Jump Start is the band's head DJ. The boy in the hat is his son. One second," she said, walking away to take her call in private.

Nneka gave me a look that let me know she'd found a new boy to entertain herself with. I knew that look well. From the fifth grade until five minutes ago, it hadn't changed. When Nneka had a crush, she really crushed!

"Look, things with Jaheir have been stale for months," she said, sighing at the mention of her on-again off-again family friend-slash-boyfriend out in Edmonton. She flipped through her WhatsApp chat to show me the string of endless memes and TikTok videos. "All social media, hardly any conversation."

"Even after the lake? Kissing under the moonlight?" I teased, referring to their encounter during his family's last trip to Toronto.

"I think I'm ready to move on," Nneka said, looking over sneakily at the boys. She fluffed up her braids and smiled.

"Well, you've definitely got some options here," I said, smiling. I wouldn't have minded an option myself.

I'd had a boyfriend in the eleventh grade, a student from St. Lucia that was in Toronto on a music exchange program. Jermaine played trombone in our school band with Omar, and joined his church band as well. He lived with one of my neighbours whose daughter was down in Castries for the exchange, so we often walked to and from school together. He was a year older than me, and while I hoped he'd stay in Toronto for university, he ended up moving back to the Caribbean to attend UWI. He was a nice boy and super Christian, so our relationship had always been extremely

G-rated. We still texted, but as friends only. I'd been single ever since.

The bass started to pump from one of the many speakers set up around the venue, followed by the orchestral sounds of the soca song playing. I moved my shoulders to the beat and pretended to sing along to the words with a flirty smile.

"Girl, you do not know these soca songs," Nneka said, rolling her eyes playfully. Neither did she, but we both laughed. "By the end of this summer we're really gonna have some new taste in music, huh?" Nneka had been heavy into the Afro-pop music coming out of Nigeria and South Africa lately.

"The music keeps the productivity up! You know I love my reggae, but when carnival time comes . . . it's *ting-ta-ting-ting* for me! High energy," Akie said, returning to sit. She pointed toward the DJ area.

"Even the DJs have a schedule!" I commented, looking at the poster board DJ Jump Start was mounting on the wall behind the music station.

"That's why Liberation is best mas band in the city!" Akie boasted.

"Akie, how do they judge that?" I asked. "I thought it was just the best costumes, but now you're telling me the DJs at the mas camp are competing too?"

Happy to answer, Akie posed with her pen mid-air.

"Let's just say that every detail matters. The costumes. The construction. Will it last all day on the parade route, or crumble and fall apart? The way all of the costumes look together as a unit. How each individual costume section looks crossing the stage. The energy. The sound on the trucks. And to get everything . . . in sync takes practice. And time spent together. Building a vibe. Building unity. It all matters in the end, and it shows."

"Whoa." Nneka exhaled. "Dem serious about this."

"All in the details," I repeated, looking around. "This'll be much more interesting than working at the park."

"Facts," Nneka agreed.

We met a few more people and even had some dinner while we worked when the lady from Caribbean Oasis restaurant showed up with a minivan filled with individual portions of stew chicken and rice. It had the familiar seasoned aroma of . . . home.

"Once you get into the groove of things, you'll be able to enjoy the vibes and atmosphere and hopefully even meet some new people," Akie told us, as her demo came to an end for the day. We all looked over at the boys.

I felt Nneka reach out to pinch my elbow. Knowing her, she'd already studied their movements, and would have a lot to chat about that evening when we got home.

CHAPTER SEVEN

Giggles and Pinches

A few weeks into May, we were already in love with the vibe at the camp. We'd wander in casually after school and on weekends and do a quick scan to see which cuties were on-site for the day. After greeting the elders and setting up our workstation, we'd find a reason to pass the DJs and say a quick hello to Jump Start and his son, Nneka's crush Rishi. He always had one or two bredrens with him. Tons of swag, all the time. Great to watch!

"Hey, Rishi," Nneka would say with a small wave whenever he passed by.

"Miss lady," he would reply with a cool nod. It was their routine. I would encourage her to go continue the conversation, but she'd always have an excuse about why she wasn't comfortable enough yet. Her stomach hurt, or she was feeling tired. She'd put it off for another day, while I was getting more and more comfortable getting friendly with Rishi's cousin Kyle and some of the others.

Kyle, a shy fella with wide brown eyes, would always wink at me with a smile.

"Miss Karla," he would say to me with a tap on my arm. He was short and cute — not my type, but it was fun to make friends and I was happy when he asked for my TikTok account after seeing me recording our progress one day.

We looked forward to our hellos and the attention from Rishi, Kyle and the friends they brought around. Everyone else at the mas camp was in their late twenties or older, so whenever teenagers passed by we got excited because they would always be drawn to us.

Akie was striking up conversations that made our workstation an inviting place to hang out — we'd chat about everything from relationships to celebrity gossip, politics and music. The weekend afternoons were chill, with DJ Jump Start or one of the other DJs on the schedule playing old calypso music or new groovy soca selections. We got familiar with the songs of the season, and sometimes even danced to ourselves while we worked, sorting and cutting materials.

Rishi was always watching us. More than the others. He

was always outside drinking, but would peek over at us from the open garage door as we worked. Nneka loved to check out his gear each day — he always had matching shoes and hats, and fresh t-shirts coordinated. She would do her makeup and style her braids extra special for the workday, wanting to stay equally fresh for her potential boo.

She was getting more and more irritable with my requests, so I stopped pressuring her about connecting with him more.

"Why you always so quiet?" Rishi asked Nneka one afternoon, passing by with a sneaky smile. "I bet you is real trouble. The quiet girls are always the bad girls."

Nneka gasped, but still managed to stay cool. "I'm just focused and I'm definitely not bad," she said confidently. I wanted to hear the rest of the conversation, but Kyle chose that moment to ask me to follow him to the backyard.

"Rishi is something else," I said to Kyle, laughing out loud. "He asked you to distract me, didn't he?"

"How'd you know?" Kyle said, taking a sip from a bottle of water he had.

"He's so obvious with it!"

"You enjoying your time here so far?" he asked, taking a seat on a plastic chair and nodding at the chair beside him for me to join him.

"It's been cool," I told him.

"How come we haven't seen allyuh around before?"

"My aunt just moved back to Toronto from Florida . . . I haven't really gone to 'Bana before."

"Really? Where your family from?"

"Jamaica. Well, my parents were born here, but my grandparents are Jamaican."

"Okay, okay."

"You?"

"Trinidad. We grew up around this. Especially with Uncle Jason . . . Jump Start," he said. "Rishi and me been around the scene since we were young."

"Do you DJ too?"

"Not yet, but I want to get more into producing and stuff," he said, smiling carefully at me. "You have a boyfriend, Karla?"

I knew the question was coming. He'd been watching me a lot lately and seemed to be working up the nerve over our last few encounters. This was the first time we'd really been alone.

"No," I said, looking around at the flow of traffic in the busy neighbourhood. The noise and activity of the camp were easily drowned out that afternoon.

"Can I get your number or Snap?"

"Sure," I said taking out my phone so we could add each other on Snapchat.

"You want me to link you next time we're going out?"

"That would be cool," I said, hoping that Rishi and Nneka were doing the same. Kyle was polite, had a cute smile, and his braids were always neat . . . he offered to share his currant roll snack with me, and after finding out he'd just finished his first year at TMU, I had a ton of questions to ask him about campus life as we ate.

A text from Nneka came in.

Nneka: I feel like I'm gonna faint fr fr

Karla: Keep it together, sis. This is your moment! Drink water and let your personality shine!

Nneka: OK I got this

***

The morning of the first official festival event, the Sunday before our Victoria Day holiday in May, Nneka called me on WhatsApp video with her entire wardrobe spread across her bed. She had been casually chatting with Rishi, but had also been getting more anxious as a result. I wasn't used to seeing her so frantic or snappy, but this crush was intense.

"What on earth am I supposed to wear?" she squealed, turning the camera from her clothing to her face as she flopped onto her bed, squeezing her eyes closed. "Everything makes me look like a whale!"

"Stop saying that," I said to her, realizing she was just a few seconds away from dropping tears. "Whale yuh gone? You've been too hard on yourself these days." Most of the time Nneka was nothing but giggles and pinches, but when she was in panic mode, I knew right away that things could go left. "I'll be there in ten."

I rode my bike to Nneka's, locking up at the side of her parents' house as I usually did. Dressed casually in a pair of black shorts and my new Liberation Mas t-shirt, I'd decided to go comfortable for the event downtown.

After greeting Mr. Obasi in the front yard, I rushed upstairs to Nneka's room, and encouraged my good sis to take a few deep breaths. I picked up her black spandex shorts and suggested we both just wear the same thing, going for a team vibe rather than a solo fashionista vibe. Nneka let out a sigh of relief, content with my quick remedy. And then she rushed to the washroom.

When she returned, I shook my head. "Nneka. You need to calm down a bit."

"Sorry, my stomach has been upset for days now," she said.

"Maybe you're worrying too much. Try not to stress!" I said to her.

"I just started thinking about Rishi, and his friends, and all of the other people across the city that will be downtown today. This is kind of a big deal," she said. I nodded in agreement. "This isn't just small talk at the mas camp, this is like, a real outing!"

"That's what this summer is for, Neeks," I told her. "And I'm pretty sure it will be exactly like the camp. Familiar faces. Please, don't worry!"

"You think they'll be downtown today? I think they will be. I'm kinda hoping they are," she said, standing up to change into her shorts. She was excited again. "You sure these don't make me look too fluffy?"

"Not even," I said immediately. "You are too cute to be this stressed. You look great now. You always look great, so let's go have fun! Did you eat breakfast already? I'm starving."

"I'm good," she said quickly. "You can grab something from the kitchen on our way, my mom fried plantain this morning."

I fixed my makeup — a subtle lipstick and some lashes — and helped Nneka pin her braids up so they wouldn't obstruct the messaging on the back of her t-shirt in pink lettering: Rosé Rendezvous.

My girl Nneka had a pretty face, flawless dark brown skin, big bright eyes and a cute nose. Her lip gloss was always popping and her lashes were naturally full and thick. She was a baddie. No matter how many times I told her that, she still thought I was just gassing her up. "It's the makeup," she'd say. "I'm too big."

I had a completely different body type. I'd always been tall and super thin, but with that thinness also came a lack of curves . . . everywhere. No hips, no waist and no chest. I had an athletic body like my mom and Akie, and could only hope to find a bit of feminine appeal one day, like the older ladies around us once we transferred from the GO train to the TTC and walked to the Liberation Mas station outside City Hall at Nathan Phillips Square. All of Toronto's masquerade bands would be stationed there for the day with presentations, registration discounts and prizes.

I saw a few familiar Toronto YouTubers in the crowd and a couple of girls I followed on TikTok. Everyone was in high spirits, with music echoing across the concrete. Akie and her models were out and about preparing for the on-stage presentation and making sure they got as many media ops as possible. Dressed in the skimpiest version of the female costumes, their bodies were on full display in the sunlight as they walked.

"Girl. Every time I see these string costumes, I panic," Nneka said, holding her hand up to her chest once we sat down at the booth. Our job was to answer questions about Akie's costume, hand out brochures and make sure our visitors scanned the

Liberation Mas QR code to register for their mailing list. "I think I'm having second thoughts . . . again. Feel my heart."

"Second thoughts . . . about what?" I asked carefully, placing my palm against her chest. We had already discussed our concerns with Akie, and now seemed to be back at square one. "Nneka, take a deep breath. This is supposed to be fun . . . don't worry so much!"

"I keep thinking about having the entire city see my fupa and back fat and stretch marks on repeat on CP24 or someone's TikTok page! The costumes look like lingerie out in the sunshine! Look at Monique . . . her body is flawless," she said, gasping as our favourite model, the bubbly and beautiful Monique began to gyrate and prance on stage in front of the deputy mayor, her long red locs swinging.

"You think he's going to be okay?" I asked Nneka, stifling a laugh as the elder politician tried to look everywhere but at the vibrant dancer's backside.

"He's probably going to have an asthma attack, and I am going to run back into my pajamas for the rest of the season," Nneka said, shaking her head. "Eh! Is Councillor Papadakos pointing his fingers in the air?" We both giggled as he started to feel the groove and dance in his seat. "Good effort, Mr. P!"

I grinned at his innocence and joy; he reminded me of my Pops.

CHAPTER EIGHT

Outside Outside

There was so much going on at the launch with music playing and food samples shared; speeches on stage and conversations with interested masqueraders going from booth to booth to collect free swag and band information kept us busy.

We were interrupted by our friends Vanessa and Tara, Filipina twin sisters from school.

“We wanted to surprise you,” Vanessa said, reaching over the booth to give us each a hug. She had her camera hanging around her neck, while Tara carried a tripod and another camera.

“We literally just decided this morning,” Tara chimed in, doing the same. They were sweet girls and always gave good energy.

"This is the costume my aunt designed," I told them, handing each girl one of the Liberation Mas brochures. "There's information about the band in here, and if you sign up for their mailing list they'll send out links to register online for costumes and event information and stuff throughout the summer."

"Is that her costume, the one on the left?" Vanessa asked, pointing to Monique in the skimpy pink Ultra Frontline costume.

"Yes, that's the one!"

"Her body is tea!" Vanessa said, gasping. "Flawless. There's options, right?"

"Plenty options," Nneka said. "You two are in great shape, you have nothing to worry about."

"So, are you two playing mas for sure for sure?" Vanessa asked. "We were thinking to give it a try . . . but it's still a lot of exposure. I mean, it's not like the beach . . . this will be on the street in front of cameras and everything."

"We were a little worried too, but my aunt says it's fine when you're there as a group and that everyone is very friendly and not there to judge," I reassured her — and Nneka. "It'll be so fun if we're all there together!"

"I think it will be a cool experience," Tara decided. "I'll definitely go to the parade, but I'll leave the costume part to Vanessa."

"As long as we're together," Vanessa agreed, and we all

cheered. "Our mom said she played mas every summer with her friends when she was a student at York."

We chatted some more about our university acceptances. Nneka and I both got into our first-choice schools, because we studied hard and didn't play about our grades, and so did the girls. They were both going to stay in the city and study close to home at U of T's Scarborough campus. Nneka was heading out to U Windsor.

As the costumed women continued to prance around the area, I could feel Nneka's confidence dimming again. While I was taking food samples at every opportunity, I noticed Nneka wasn't even eating. She was in her head and I knew I'd have to try to lift her spirits.

We promised our parents we'd be home before it got dark. As the sun started to dip, we helped Akie pack the contents of her booth and bring everything down to her car in the underground parking garage. She walked with us back to the subway entrance.

"Thank you for your help today! I've been here over twelve hours and probably won't leave for a few more," Akie said, exhausted but happy. "Now . . . it's time to unwind!"

"Have fun, Auntie!" Nneka said, hugging her quickly. Akie pulled back to look at us both carefully.

"What happened? Are you guys okay?" She looked at me

closely, then back to Nneka. "Was anyone rude to you? Are you hungry? What's going on? Is it because you have to leave early?" I looked at Nneka, who shrugged as Akie handed her the small packet of oatmeal cookies she had in her purse. "You look weak, Nneka! I thought you guys would be out enjoying all the free food samples!" Nneka hesitated at first, but ate the cookies quickly.

"The costumes look amazing," Nneka began after a few deep breaths. Now that Akie mentioned it, she did look kinda frail. "All of them. They looked so good on stage at the band launch, they look good on display in the mas camp. Even in the Instagram photos and the website." She paused. "But out here in the bright-ass sun, Auntie! With every single blemish and body part exposed? We have to wear these costumes *outside* outside! And around strangers! Thousands of them. This is all a little bit too real now and I'm panicking because I'm a lil fluffy and I don't need everyone out there to see exactly how fluffy I am."

Akie sighed and shook her head sadly. "Come on, Nneka, girl. Look at that bumpa," she teased, tapping her lightly on her thigh. "Last I checked, women were paying money to get the shape you were naturally born with. You're a beautiful girl and have nothing to worry about: *strong body*, as the Caribbean man dem would say!"

We both hollered — Akie always knew how to make us giggle!

"*Strong body*," Nneka repeated, laughing. "It's just a lot . . ." she said carefully.

"I know, babes," Akie said, hugging Nneka to her side. "But hear me and hear me good. You are beautiful. You are both beautiful and always have been. You're both extremely smart and kind. I don't want to force you to participate, but I want to remind you that you will most likely have an amazing time. After all the work you've put in, I would love to have you there to celebrate the carnival in full costume — that I will customize for you, by the way — so you can get the full experience. Wearing the costume is an important part. The liberation! The freedom! Taking over the streets and dancing and feeling confident no matter what size you are. That's my wish for you . . . but I don't want to pressure you either."

"Real talk though, Akie. We are going from wearing joggers and t-shirts every day to basically prancing around downtown in our underwear!" I said. "I understand that we should be confident . . . but . . . this is a big jump for us."

"I don't want to put you in an uncomfortable position, so . . . what I had in mind for you . . ." Akie began, looking at me, "was some hot shorts and a crop top," she said, motioning at her own body to show me just how short and how cropped. "I know your mom will appreciate that too." Akie hugged me. "I'm not going to force you, but I do hope that getting caught up in the momentum and the excitement will help. It's going to be a great experience, you have to trust me on this one."

"Okay . . ." Nneka said, smiling in relief.

"For you," Akie said, placing her hands on her hips, "I will create a full corset top, a lil' revealing around here," her hands hovered over her chest. "But fully covered around here," she motioned around her midsection and back. "Very cutesy. I'll give you longer spandex shorts, add a lil' chiffon with your fabric for accents on the belt. It'll be light, it'll flow, and you'll be totally covered."

Her descriptions comforted us and we didn't want to delay her well-deserved partying, so I reassured Akie that we'd be okay and linked arms with Nneka to head toward the subway. We arrived at Union Station just in time to catch our GO train, and went on our phones to catch up on the posts and memes we missed during the day.

Nneka complained about feeling nauseous, and rested her head in her hands for most of the trip, too queasy to chat or scroll. We were both relieved to arrive back in Scarborough.

"How about next summer we work with a Nigerian organization so we can cover up our bodies and not have to stress about this special tailoring?" Nneka said, as we stood waiting for Ekene to pick us up from the station. Her mother had insisted. "The African events are more about the music, and food and crafts. Your people are fun . . . but too much pressure."

"Wha' gwan, Ekene?" I asked, jumping in the back seat as he arrived, trying to process Nneka's dig.

"Hey, Karla. You two have fun?" he asked, heading toward our neighbourhood at Meadowvale and Ellesmere.

"Karla's carnival community has me signing up to put on panties and a bra so tourists can take pictures of me fully exposed in the bright sunshine." Nneka sighed dramatically. I knew she was in her feelings, but thought she was being unnecessarily salty. Especially since Akie had just offered to build her a customized version of Rosé Rendezvous. "Caribbean people love show off dey nyash."

"Whoa, whoa!" I said, laughing in disbelief. I couldn't believe she was still going on about this, like she wasn't practically raised in my Caribbean household too. "I'm not any more comfortable with this than you are. I just thought it would be fun."

"Did someone say nyash? Plenty nyash down at Nathan Phillips Square tonight?" Ekene asked us both. "I'm picking up Anthony after and we were going to head down there for the performances."

I let him know about the countless beautiful women prancing around the Square wrapped in decorated strings and feathers, trying to keep the vibe light before I said something I regretted.

"So what's the problem, sis? Obviously there's a reason so many women, of all sizes from what I've seen, sign up for the parade every year," Ekene said.

"Caribbean people love this kind of spectacle. Maybe I need to cover my Nigerian butt in something traditional, like a wrapper. This isn't right for me," Nneka said. Yup, she was definitely in a mood, and I was officially offended.

"Nneka, are you being serious right now? A wrapper? Plus, it's not like my family grew up in this type of culture, or my parents would even accept any bad behaviour or exposure from me! My grandparents are Christians, just like yours. Your parents and my parents grew up in Scarborough, just like us, and this is more of a Toronto thing than an 'island people ting' at this point. You guys haven't even been to Nigeria in like ten years, so you need to calm down."

I didn't know how else to respond. I didn't like to argue with Nneka, and I wasn't going to do anything to upset her even more. She'd started off the day sad, and I didn't want to make it worse.

"Honestly. It's probably going to be a lot of fun for you two — the music and dancing. You two need to see Dad's videotapes from Caribana days. Hilarious."

"Ekene's right, all these girls wouldn't participate if it wasn't amazing," I said, shrugging. I was now in *my* feelings and ready to get out of the car. Nneka knew how hard we had been working . . . and now wanted to attack me for how she was feeling? It wasn't fair.

"I dunno, Karla. Prancing around Toronto half-naked and calling it culture?" she said, rolling her eyes and folding her arms across her seatbelt.

"Nneka! What the eff? Are you being for real right now?" I was shocked at how far she was taking the insult. "People in Toronto have been doing this for decades . . . you know the history and you know very well that this is a big deal for the Caribbean community. And Akie! That was rude . . ." I said, kissing my teeth. "If Tara and Vanessa can show respect for a cultural tradition, why can't you?"

Her words stung. I wanted to cry but held back my tears. "Thanks, Ekene," I said when we arrived at my house. He gave me an apologetic shrug. I didn't even look at Nneka before shutting the door, and I wouldn't send or respond to her messages that night. She had taken things too far.

Kyle texted me to let me know he had just arrived downtown with Rishi and their friends, but I told him we'd already returned to the east. I knew he was disappointed that we wouldn't get to hang and party together, but the way I was feeling, I was glad to be home to relax. I distracted myself watching videos on TMU's YouTube page until I fell asleep.

CHAPTER NINE

Jollof Rice and Peas

"You good, Karla?" my dad asked me when I returned from school alone on Friday evening. Usually I'd be with Nneka, but she disappeared after the bell. He knew our regular routine but didn't press me for an explanation.

"Yes, Daddy," I said, welcoming the beef patty, soft coco bread and side of plantain chips he handed me when I entered the kitchen. He was sitting down to have his own snack and noticed my long face.

"Kola Champagne or pineapple?" he asked, holding up two cold soft drinks.

"Pineapple, please!" I said, taking the glass bottle from him.

"About one more week of class before exams, huh?"

"Yeah. I feel prepared, though," I said, taking the plate and nodding toward the stairs. "I'm gonna eat in my room before I head out to help Akie."

"Okay," Dad said, picking up his phone. "Lemme know if you want more chips before I eat them all. I think I'll FaceTime Dorian and see what he has going on for the weekend. Probably going to the beach or uptown Kingston to some fancy day party, as usual."

"Most likely! Thanks, Daddy," I said, heading upstairs to worry.

I wasn't good. Things had been weird with Nneka at school all week. We didn't ask one another any questions throughout the day to check in, and found other things to do during lunch hour, when we would usually connect. It was awkward, but neither of us was ready to talk about our summer plans.

I was an honorary Nigerian the same way she was an honorary Jamaican. We shared foods and music; our families knew about each other's native countries because of how close we were. We enjoyed jollof rice and they loved rice and peas. We used each other's slang and were proud of our shared heritage as West African descendants.

We also both grew up in Scarborough in the same neighbourhood, and were both as Canadian as our friends from all backgrounds. We knew about Filipino lumpia, how to dance to Punjabi music, and went ice skating and did

Canadian things growing up. I knew it, and Nneka knew it. She was being facety, as the Jamaicans would say, or as the Nigerians would say, she no dey behave.

Nneka: So you're mad at me?

Nneka's text broke the ice, but I was still angry.

Karla: Mad? I'm hurt.

Nneka: I was just kidding. Whatever it was that I said that hurt you, I was joking.

Karla: Why would u even joke about something like that? Especially now? This is our summer job. This is supposed to be fun. Akie has invested so much into her section and into our help. Why are you messing with that? Plus, I have never ever disrespected Nigerian people or African culture.

Nneka: I wasn't disrespecting your culture.

Karla: You were literally taking jabs at island people all day. Every comment you made, Caribbean people were catching strays.

Nneka: Well sorry then.

Karla: Is that supposed to be an apology?

Tired of texting, I FaceTimed her and waited for her to pick up. Nneka was lying in bed; her face looked grey. She didn't look well at all, but my concern for her health wasn't as strong as my disappointment in her attitude.

"I don't feel good," Nneka said, closing her eyes but keeping the camera steady.

"Badmind will do that to you," I replied. "Nneka, no one forced you to do 'Bana with me. This is something we've heard both of our parents talk about, and Dorian, and Ekene, and we always thought it would be fun. So why all of a sudden you wanna act like there's something wrong here? Where's your loyalty?"

"I was just saying Caribbean culture focuses on the wining up and exposing bodies in a way Nigerian culture doesn't."

"Maybe that's part of the culture, but you have been through enough with my family and our friends to know better. Why would you come for me like that?"

"I wasn't coming for you, I just was saying I would be more comfortable doing something more . . . respectable."

"Nneka! What? That's rude!"

"Think about it. The way the ladies are dancing around practically naked . . . not everyone is going to think it's some deep cultural moment. They're going to see it and immediately think it's sexy and sexual."

"What are you even saying?" I said, trying not to raise my voice and alarm my dad.

"I'm just saying . . . it is what it is."

"You're wrong," I said to her, watching her shrug. Tears sprang to my eyes, and my throat tightened, but I wasn't going to let her see me cry. "What is going on with you? It's like you're an entirely different person all of a sudden. You've been so freakin' irritable, and this is supposed to be fun, remember? We're supposed to meet new people and mingle with these dudes and carry on this summer. Why are you ruining this?"

"Look, I'm sorry," Nneka said. She was clearly tired and wasn't giving our argument the energy it deserved. "I was out of line, and I'm sorry. I'm sure we'll still have fun this summer."

"Are you sure about that? Because you're flopping the vibes."

"Sorry. I was reading some stuff and watching some videos about the original Caribana, and all the changes the parade went through, and it didn't feel like it was focused on the original purpose. Like, I get it, the emancipation and celebration. I get it. But Karla . . . you saw those costumes. And those beautiful women. How else was I supposed to feel?"

"You're supposed to trust that Akie wouldn't bring us to do something harmful," I started slowly. "And why should we be concerned about all the mix-up with the organizers? Like, do you want to jump up or nah?"

"I hear you . . ." Nneka sighed, giving in. "It's just not what I was expecting."

"What more would you want?" I asked her genuinely. "Can we not just try to learn and enjoy it as much as possible? This time next year who knows where we'll be."

"I hear you . . ." she said again. "I'm sorry I was rude. I just . . . I just saw those supermodels and the boys, and I guess I got intimidated."

"Nneka, you have been the most outgoing and likeable person I've known ever since we met. Don't start to doubt that now. Let's just embrace the experience and try to have fun. Please!"

"Sorry, Karla. I don't want to ruin your fun."

"Thank you!"

"Please tell Akie I'll be back as soon as I feel better. I'm gonna nap, okay?"

"Okay, Neeks. Feel better."

***

Without Nneka around the mas camp that Friday evening, I focused on my cutting and sorting and double-checked our notes to make sure everything was in order. Kyle came by to chat with me briefly when him and Rishi passed by the workstation. They were coming to invite me and Nneka to a blocko that night, but I let them know she wasn't feeling well and I wasn't comfortable rolling solo.

I immediately missed Nneka being there, and hated that she'd missed out on the invitation to hang with the guys.

"How's Nneka doing? She okay?" Akie asked, noticing how quiet I was.

"She's okay. I think the carnival scene is overwhelming her . . ."

"She's still worried about the costume," Akie guessed. I nodded, and she sighed.

I gestured around us. "This scene is a vibe. And Nneka feels like it's all about being sexy and dancing in costume and it might be scaring her away a bit. At school everyone loves her personality, and she's obviously very pretty. But exposure like this has never been an issue."

Akie let out another deep sigh and took off her glasses for a moment. She put down her scissors and took my hand. "Does she want to quit?"

"I don't think so. She didn't say anything . . . but she did say a few things about Caribbean culture," I confessed. "She thinks we're too focused on booties and exposure and maybe it's not what she expected. I dunno."

"Booties and exposure? She said that?" Akie exhaled slowly before kissing her teeth, extremely unimpressed. She shook her head slowly. "She should know better."

"She does," I said to her carefully. "I don't think she was trying to be rude, but she keeps having second thoughts."

"I'm pretty sure I remember her mom Francine getting on bad back in the day at one or two blockos." Akie shrugged, rolling her eyes. "Nneka doesn't realize this is in her genes as much as it's in ours? That it's a celebration? She should know this."

"Nneka said her parents met at a soca fete in the nineties . . . I mean, they grew up in Toronto too, so they're not new to Caribana. Auntie Francine even used to play mas back in the day."

"I would never bring you into something I didn't think was going to benefit you. Maybe I'll give her a ring, and let's just deal with this right now before it develops into something worse."

"We chatted a bit before I came, and she apologized," I said. "It's not like her to even mention stuff like this."

Akie was calling Nneka before I could even finish the sentence.

"Eh, likkle gyal," Akie said, giving Nneka a screwface when

she appeared on the screen. I knew she'd be shocked, because Akie was never mean.

"Hi, Auntie Akilah," Nneka said sheepishly.

"Karla says you a diss we people and we culture?" Akie got right to the point.

"I know . . . I shouldn't have said what I said."

"Why did you say those things, babes?" Akie kept her face stern.

"I dunno."

"You don't wanna help out or play mas with us anymore?"

"I do . . ."

"So what's happening? Talk to me. Let me help you get through this funk, because it should never *ever* get to the point where you're talking down to your sister."

"I know . . ."

"You girls have been friends for like, what, almost fifteen years?"

"Yes, Auntie."

"You are in this world together and can't afford to fight each other over small cultural differences."

"You're right."

"Whether you're from Ghana or St. Vincent or born in Canada like you two, we are all one, okay? Please don't ever let your mind trick you into believing anything else."

"Yes, Auntie," Nneka said, and even without seeing her face I knew she was embarrassed.

I opened up my pink sewing kit to grab a few safety pins and my scissors so I could assist with the rest of the cutting, including Nneka's share.

CHAPTER TEN

One Love

I texted Nneka after she got off the phone with Akie.

Karla: Rishi and Kyle stopped by to invite us to a blocko tonight.

Nneka: Omg for real

Karla: Yupppppppp

I inserted a few rows of "thumbs down" emojis to express my disappointment.

Nneka: Not good.

Karla: Nope.

Nneka: Girl, I'm sorry. I don't know what got into me, and I hated not being at the mas camp. I definitely don't wanna be stuck here watching Nollywood movies with my dad every night.

Karla: So be for real . . . what's the problem? Because I know it's not Caribbean culture. When you were with Jaheir you never had an issue with it and he was as Caribbean as it gets.

Nneka: I know. It was a low blow. And I didn't mean to leave you hanging at work tonight, but I'm a mess.

Karla: How u feelin

Nneka: Like garbage. I haven't really eaten all week.

Nneka: I've been so nauseous and tired.

Karla: Well get some rest and we'll talk tomorrow.

Nneka: You don't hate me?

Karla: Impossible

Nneka: And Akie

Karla: She loves you.

Karla: But just remember we're on the same team. Don't turn us into the enemy, there's a bigger picture ya know?

Nneka: I know.

Karla: Look, we both agreed this would be an amazing experience and I want us to see it through.

Nneka: Aright. Lemme focus. I can do this.

Karla: We can totally do this. Is no scene. I just learned that today: no scene.

Nneka: Ok. Call me after. And "One Love" my Caribbean sistren.

Karla: Don't be corny heheh

***

"Tell me everything," Nneka said on video chat after Akie dropped me home around ten; she stayed downstairs to chat with Mom and Daddy.

"Rishi and Kyle came right to me as soon as they got to the camp," I began.

"What was he wearing?"

"Jeans and green. Lots of green today. And he had a fresh braid up," I told her. "They wanted us to roll."

"Ughhh!" she said, dramatically — but silently — banging her desk. "Do you think it's too late for us to go?"

"There's no way my dad will agree to us going out this late."

"Same."

Nneka showed me the flat carnival boots she ordered online to match our costumes that summer. "I got a pair for you too."

"I'm a lil' nervous about the exposure too, but Akie's modifications look okay. It'll just be like wearing shorts and a tank," I said to her.

"Literally," she agreed. "I think I just needed someone or something to blame. I was in my feelings."

"It's all good, okay? School's almost out. First, we'll ace our exams, and then we'll focus on this experience."

"Yes, we will live in the moment. Uh, my stomach still hurts. All week I've been feeling bloated."

"Damn, all week?" I said.

"I think I'm gonna throw up. I'll link you back," Nneka said, rushing off the phone.

CHAPTER ELEVEN

Road March

The first two weekends in June, after studying for exams, we spent the evenings with Akie entering registrations into her database and taking measurements of the masqueraders that came in to purchase costumes. We didn't see much of Rishi and Kyle, who were out partying from the looks of their social media. Even the twins popped by; we walked them through each piece selection, showing them examples as Akie listened in proudly. Vanessa was ready to register, but Tara was still firm in her decision to join us in just her street clothes.

My bestie was inspired again. "Let's go to the camp," Nneka said over the phone. It was Sunday afternoon; our last day of exams was coming up. We weren't on the schedule for the camp. She was obviously unable to focus.

"Girl, what about the English exam?" I had to ask.

"I know, I know . . . let's just pop in for a bit and see what's happening," she said. I saw a notification on my phone and opened her WhatsApp message to see a screenshot of Rishi's Instagram page, showing him looking out at the warehouse from behind his dad's laptop.

"Ahh, I see," I said, acknowledging the photo. "The coast is clear?"

"I think it's a good time to really talk to him," Nneka concluded. "I'm gonna ask Ekene to drive us. We don't have to stay long. Like twenty minutes," she pleaded. I couldn't say no, and she knew it. "I'll text you when we're outside."

The Liberation team greeted us as we approached our workstation with warm smiles and waves. Ekene was hanging out in the front parking lot talking to a girl he knew and her friends. Rishi was slim but tall. Cute and confident. Maybe even a little cocky. Kyle saw the play and sent me a quick text. We had been sending TikToks and checking in with each other regularly. Nothing serious though.

Kyle: Come over, nah?

Karla: omw

I knew Nneka was nervous.

I nodded for Nneka to join me in going over to them. I walked over casually and she followed behind.

"Wha' gwan," Kyle said, reaching out to give me and Nneka a friendly hug.

"Hey, Kyle. Rishi," I said with a wave. "How you guys doing?"

"Good, good," Kyle said. Nneka and Rishi stood awkwardly around each other. "Come, let's go outside." Kyle took control of the situation, and we followed. I felt Nneka pinch my arm as we walked.

Kyle pulled up four chairs for us to sit in a shaded area next to a wall out back. I could hear Ekene cracking jokes with his lady friends and figured he wouldn't mind the minor delay.

"You want a drink?" Rishi asked Nneka, taking a small bottle of rum and a stack of cups out of his backpack.

"Sure, I'll have a sip," she said.

"You?" Rishi asked me. I shook my head.

"I'm good," I said, holding up the bottle of water I had with me.

Rishi was prepared! He poured a cup of rum and Coke for my girl, and even went into the camp to get her some ice. He handed it to her with pride. "Let me know if it's okay."

Nneka took a sip and smiled. "Yes, thank you." I knew she was nervous, but she still looked confident and beautiful.

"So you two don't party?" Rishi asked. "I don't ever see you out. Just here."

"Not really . . ." I told him. "Where do you usually go?"

"In the summer we usually just chill on some house party backyard vibes, or see what blockos are happening," Kyle said.

"Or we just lime, just so," Rishi added, outstretching his arms. "My kinda t'ing."

Nneka looked giddy, sipping her drink and trying not to wince.

"You nineteen yet?" Rishi asked Nneka with a grin.

"Not until February," she said bashfully. "You?"

"I just turned nineteen the other day," he told her. I already knew that Kyle was still nineteen from our chats.

"What song you think gonna get Road March in Toronto this year?" Kyle asked me. I shrugged, smiling in embarrassment.

"I swear I know most of the new soca now, but not everything. I'm still getting familiar . . ." I defended myself.

"Ah, what about you?" Rishi asked, already refilling his cup. "Yuh listen soca?"

"I do . . ." Nneka said, shyly.

"Nah, I don't believe that," he teased her, reaching out to pat her leg. "I'm gonna get you up to speed before the parade."

Of course, the moment they connected, we saw Ekene come around the corner. He tapped his watch when he caught my eye. Nneka couldn't see him, so I nodded for her attention.

"Dat your man?" Rishi asked Nneka immediately. "The guy that drove you here?"

"My brother."

"Okay . . . okay," he said, relieved.

"He's our ride home," she said, taking a longer sip. I knew she wasn't an experienced drinker, but was trying to act the part for Rishi's sake.

"Ten minutes," Ekene called out to us. I gave him a thumbs up.

Nneka shook her head quickly. I noticed her eyes were heavy; she didn't look good and was beginning to slightly sway in her seat. "We'll be right back," I said to the boys, taking Nneka's arm and walking with her back into the camp.

"Girl, you okay?" I asked.

"Walk with me to that room with the sofa, low-key. I feel like I'm going to faint," she said, putting her cup in the garbage. I linked my arm through hers and guided her to the room. She sat on the couch and her head immediately fell back.

"Nneka!" I said to her, shaking her lightly. I looked around the room and there were cases of water stacked in the corner. I took a bottle and held it to help her drink. "Maybe you need to eat something! You want me to grab two cookies from Akie? What's going on? The rum?"

She opened her eyes, blinked in confusion a few times and shook her head. Taking the bottle from me, Nneka sipped the water and continued to take deep breaths.

"I feel a little nauseous. My cycle's been weird lately. Maybe it's that," she said, resting her head in her hands. "Let's go say bye to Rishi and Kyle," she said hesitantly. "Ekene's probably ready to go anyhow. Can we go chill at your house and study there? I need a nap first, but I don't want my parents to see me sleeping in the day."

"Of course. Let's go," I said. "You sure you're okay?" I double-checked, looking in her eyes.

"Yeah, I'm good," she said.

CHAPTER TWELVE
Dainty Girl

I reviewed my study notes while Nneka lay on my bed. Kyle was disappointed we had to leave and had been texting me all afternoon. Rishi was sharing YouTube video links with Nneka, trying to get her used to the big songs of the carnival season. We were both saddened that we had to cut our little time short, but happy Kyle and Rishi were still connecting with us.

"You have cramps?" I asked, sitting beside Nneka and resting my hand on her forehead. "You've been dizzy all week, now that I think about it. And I've never seen you faint before. Like, ever."

"I'll be fine. End-of-the-semester stress, maybe? Plus, I've been thinking a lot about moving to Windsor . . ." she said, shrugging, nestling into my pillow and closing her eyes. "I hope those guys wanna hang out again soon."

"For sure they will," I said, showing her the long text messages Kyle was sending me. "Kyle is jokes! Plus, we'll be back on Wednesday. Exams over and stress-free!"

"Hey, look at this," Nneka said, taking a packet of Dainty Girl Tea out of her bag. "I thought it would give me energy to be more productive this summer and even lose a little weight. I wonder if this is making me feel sick?"

I quickly read the back of the package and remembered seeing influencer-paid ads showcasing it on TikTok.

"Neeks, this can't be good!" I exclaimed, tilting my head as I studied the neon green branding. "All these roots and oils . . . it's practically a laxative! No wonder you're not feeling well!" I opened TikTok and typed the name into the search bar, looking for the packaging. The videos I found were mainly a string of teen girls complaining about side effects from the tea; posts about fainting, dizzy spells, dehydration, bloating and digestive issues flooded my timeline before anything positive did.

"Oh snap!" Nneka said, after the fifth video played. Each girl described her symptoms and cussed the product. I scrolled through a few more AI-generated video testimonials while Nneka bowed her head in shame.

"You might want to reconsider this," I told her carefully,

placing the packet down on the bed. Nneka's eyes began to well up. "Let's start walking after exams. Or try some dancing or group fitness? Maybe one of those soca exercise classes so we can get familiar with the songs too?"

"That sounds good," she said. "I know better. I should have researched this properly."

"Please know that you're already perfect," I reassured her. "Don't let the costume pressure stress you. Remember Akie said that when all of the costumes are together on the road, people won't notice what we think are our little flaws. They'll just be overwhelmed by the beauty of the costumes and the energy we bring."

"I know, I know. But this," she said, pointing to her belly, slightly round and disguised under a t-shirt. "Every time I think about going to talk to Rishi, I feel every single roll. I have never felt this insecure about my weight before . . . but now!" She sighed. "I thought a little detox would help and then I could take it from there," she said, placing her hand to her forehead and closing her eyes.

"How you feeling now? Do you want to maybe call your doctor or see if my parents can bring you to the walk-in clinic?"

She shook her head. "Girl, if my parents know that I'm not well, they'll find a way to make this a reason for me to stay home all summer," she concluded. I had to agree. The less our parents knew about our side missions, the better.

"Okay, well, can I at least make you some proper lunch and get you a ginger ale to settle your stomach? You can rest and I'll read through the notes out loud."

"Sounds like a plan," she said, keeping her eyes closed. I went to the kitchen to prepare leftovers and a cold glass of soda. Nneka was sleeping when I got back upstairs, so I left her food on a tray at my desk, got comfy on my small area rug and continued to quiz myself on the novels and grammar rules we'd reviewed in English class.

I was worried about Nneka.

She may have felt too big, but I felt I was too flat up top and down below. Boring, boring, boring. I was afraid that no amount of feathers and bling would make me look like a sexy carnivalista. That I'd still look like nerdy-but-pleasant Karla.

I wasn't going to let my fear get in the way of the fun, though, and I needed Nneka to understand that too. We had to stop focusing on our bodies in costumes and concentrate on the parade day and the full summer experience.

Plus, there was still a lot of beading and gluing to do.

We ate lunch together after Nneka woke up from her brief nap and sat cross-legged on my bedroom carpet with me to finish studying.

My dad came up to my room to check on me after Nneka went home for the night.

"All ready for the exam tomorrow?" he asked, nodding at the laptop.

"Yes, sir!" I said to him. "Come, let me tell you about all of these exciting literary terms and styles!"

"Okay," he said, taking a seat at my desk chair. "Spoken like a girl who's about to ace that test!"

CHAPTER THIRTEEN
Graduation

Hours before our graduation ceremony, I met Nneka at our favourite spot in the school cafeteria: a cozy corner by the window where we usually linked up with our girls before and after class. She was sipping from a Tim Hortons cup and seemed to be back to her regular diet.

"Can you believe we won't have to sit in this caf again?" she said, pulling a hot chocolate out of a cupholder for me. She waved over at Chelsea, who entered the room with her parents.

"I'll kinda miss it," I said, nodding in thanks as I took a sip.

"Yeah, I'll miss getting to see you guys every day," she agreed, waving at our friends Angela and Tania, who we'd known since elementary. I smiled at them, and they came over to chill.

"So you guys are really doing 'Bana?" Angela asked, clapping her hands.

"Ya, my aunt makes costumes, so we're working with her to help out."

"Oh wow, that's cool," said Tania, sitting down and resting her chin on her hands.

"Do you think they'd let us be in the parade too?" Angela asked. "Like, do you have to pay to get in, or audition?"

"Pay yes, audition, no," Nneka said. "You pay for your costume, pick out the section and style you want and then we build them. On carnival day you put on the costume from home, we meet up downtown at the CNE as a unit . . . and we hit the parade route for judging."

"Seriously? I thought the dancers had to audition!" Angela said, her eyes widening with possibility. "So basically anyone can join?"

"Pretty much," Nneka told her. "I mean, the costumes are pricey, but if you can pay for it . . . you're in!"

"How pricey?" Tania wondered.

"They range from like four hundred to about fourteen hundred," Nneka said, pulling up the Liberation Mas website on her phone. "Here, I'll send you the link so you can see the breakdown."

"Fourteen hundred!" Angela was in awe. "Girl, that is a

lot of money for a little panty and bra. My brother just got a decent car that only cost him twelve g's!"

"That's what we thought at first," I told her. "But once you look at the price of materials plus all the work it takes to make the costumes, it makes sense."

"Okay, I could see that being expensive," Tania said, looking at the link Nneka shared. "Can we visit you over there to check it out?"

"Most definitely," I told her. We'll practically be there every day for the rest of the month, and for all of July."

Mom texted to let me know that she and Daddy were already seated in the auditorium. Nneka's parents joined them shortly after while we listened to instructions from our principal, reviewed the evening's agenda and arranged ourselves in line alphabetically.

Dorian: Congratulations sis! Enjoy graduation night! You going to any parties afterward?

Karla: Ya our friend Omar is having people over. He has a pool.

Dorian: Word

Dorian: Have fun. Dad's already sending me pics so he'll probably start livestreaming for us once you guys enter the auditorium. We're practically there with you.

Karla: Thanks bro bro. Gotta line up now.

Dorian: OK, Gran and Pops said they're proud of you!

CHAPTER FOURTEEN
Thirst Traps

"What do you think about dark pink braids?" Nneka asked, turning the screen of her phone to show me a young lady with a similarly round face shape and deep complexion. "Just the ends."

"Pink is pretty," I said, nodding as I opened my sewing kit. We took the day after graduation off but were back at the camp for Thursday evening. Nneka's energy was up, and I made sure we had a good lunch that afternoon.

"So, I decided today's the day," she said, showing Rishi's TikTok page to me. "He's been liking my videos and stuff, but we haven't really been messaging. So I'm gonna ask him out. On a date."

"Lemme see," I said, scrolling through his videos on her

phone and skimming his captions. "He's definitely single and he wants everyone to know."

"Right? Major thirst traps. And they're working," she said, giggling. "I love when he takes his braids out. His hair's so curly and soft and nice."

"He's a cutie and seemed to enjoy your company last week," I encouraged her. He hadn't arrived at the camp yet, and a local radio station was playing through the speakers. No live DJs.

Nneka took her phone from me and exited the app. "Scurred."

"Don't be! Look, I saw some fruits in the kitchen. I'll get us some; I'll be right back." I stood up to get some snacks before we got into our work.

"Can you bring me my little lunch bag when you go? I left it in there on my way to the washroom."

After filling a plastic bowl with grapes and melon pieces for us to share, I spotted Nneka's lunch bag and picked it up. My hands were full with the fruits, two plastic forks and some napkins, so I opened the bag to put some things in before walking back to our workstation.

Not only was Nneka still storing packets of the Dainty Girl Tea, but the bag also contained weight-loss gummies and even some over-the-counter laxatives. I had to be nosy. I checked the packing slip and it had just arrived that morning. Also listed: two waist trainers and lotion for removing stretch marks.

I didn't even know what to say when I returned with her bag and matching water bottle hanging from the side. I was stunned that her weight had been on her mind this much. Growing up, it was barely an issue because everyone just loved her for being her. I didn't want to blame Rishi, but felt like he was the main reason she wanted to change her appearance. Along with the costumes.

"Thanks!" Nneka smiled, taking a sip from her water bottle.

Deciding to put Nneka's supplements and everything else out of my mind until we left the camp, I did my best to go through the afternoon without mentioning the items. As long as she was eating and staying hydrated, I left it alone.

"Wha' gwan?" I heard Rishi's familiar voice from behind. He tapped my shoulder and also squeezed Nneka's as he walked past us, pausing to give Akie a quick kiss on her cheek. Akie was on a call with Jamar and had her ear pods in for the past hour, focused on her beading.

"Hey," I said casually with a smile. He was alone, but I knew Kyle was planning to stop by that evening too.

"Hey, Rishi," Nneka said confidently, also grinning.

“Yuh good?” he asked her, flashing the smile that we’d be talking about all night.

“Yeah, I’m okay,” she said with a perfect pretty Nneka smile. How could he not be interested in her? Rishi continued on to the DJ station where his dad had just arrived and was setting up.

A group of girls dressed in matching white workout sets entered through the back door and laid a few yoga mats on the concrete. They gathered around DJ Jump Start, complaining about the overcast weather.

“For those of you who registered for CalypsoYoga this evening,” Jump Start said on the microphone, echoing throughout the mas camp, “class will be held inside today because of the weather.”

“CalypsoYoga?” Nneka repeated.

I looked over at the slender ladies as they stretched and prepared for their class. Their bodies were snatched. I recognized a few of them from the website, modelling the costumes with ease. Even the barely there string options.

“I don’t know if I can do that . . . here!” I said quietly, looking at one girl stretching in front of Rishi. He didn’t even try to hide his amusement.

While the costume making continued, the yoga class also went on along with some construction in the back of the warehouse where a group of older men were building the floats for the upcoming King and Queen competition.

Our first day at the camp post-graduation, we tried to keep up with the quota on Akie's schedule and make sure we cut all the fabrics for the belts. Our next step would be to group the belts according to size and label them for specific masqueraders.

We didn't want to make any mistakes, so we worked carefully and quietly until we were in a comfortable groove. The CalypsoYoga crew finished their class and were prancing and giggling around the warehouse, capturing the attention of all the young males in the room — including Rishi. Nneka didn't mention her plan to ask him out, but instead kept her head down, focused on her tasks.

We were both exhausted. Kyle was a no-show and Rishi was still being entertained by the CalypsoYoga girls. When my dad came to pick us up, we waved to a few team members around us before heading out to his car. He dropped Nneka off and then we went to grab ice cream before heading home. Dad brought Mom a sundae and sat next to her on the couch where she was reading to catch up on his Netflix shows for the night.

CHAPTER FIFTEEN

Innocent Smile

I sent Nneka a few TikTok videos, but otherwise we didn't chat much for the night. I think we were both exhausted from our detailed tasks, realizing the volume we had ahead of us for the summer. I didn't ask about the Rishi plan, and Kyle explained to me that he had to help his mom with something and couldn't make it out.

The next day, Nneka texted me in the morning to say she wasn't feeling good and wouldn't be able to work as planned. I didn't know what to think, but decided to let her rest and focus on getting both of our jobs done.

Akie picked me up and we had a nice afternoon together, singing along to the R&B oldies playing through the camp. It was like a choir in the room with the women singing and dancing in their seats as they worked. I wished Nneka could be there with us, and decided to ride my bike over to her place after Akie dropped me home in the early evening.

Mr. Obasi let me in, and I sat carefully on the edge of Nneka's bed. Her usually clear complexion seemed dull and dry. She was not okay.

"Hey," she said, stirring when she noticed me sitting with her.

"Okay, what is going on?" I said, keeping my voice low so Ekene couldn't hear us in the next room. "Nneka! Are you still taking those crazy diet potions? You never, ever get sick this much, girl. I'm worried!" I said, looking at the small bucket she had next to her bed.

"I'm getting these sharp pains in my stomach," she said. A tear slid down to her pillow while she looked blankly ahead of her. "I've lost ten pounds this week . . ."

"Ten pounds! Nneka!" I said, kneeling at the bed beside her and resting my hand on her shoulder. "This can't be good, what are you doing? Why is this suddenly an issue for you?"

"I'm worried about the costume still . . ."

"Come on. That's not even a good enough reason anymore, because Akie said she'd give us exactly what we asked for to feel comfortable. We're not holding you hostage to do this either and Akie's not pressuring us," I said, frustrated and confused. And scared. "Did I miss something?"

"I texted Rishi," she said, and tears continued to leak from her eyes. She paused, moaned and leaned over to vomit in the bucket — mainly water. I handed her the small towel on her dresser and placed my hand on her forehead. It felt cool and she was shivering.

"Should I get your dad?"

"Please . . . don't. He won't understand."

"Nneka, I don't even understand!"

"I haven't eaten today, okay. I just had the tea. And the laxative. And they're both working . . . too well," she said, resting the cloth on her face. "I have never hated the way I look this much, but I can't stop thinking about it now."

"Nneka!" I said, my own tears beginning to form. "If you want to take a break from the 'Bana stuff to focus on your health I'll understand, and so will Akie. This is messing with your mind!"

"No, I need the money to save up for the fall . . . and I really want to experience this with you."

"Not like this," I said to her, sitting down on her desk chair. "You're freaking me out and you need to explain what's triggering you. What did Rishi say?" I asked, looking at her sad eyes. "No one should lose that much weight that quickly, and plus . . . I saw all those things in your bag the other day," I admitted. "Rishi or no Rishi . . . this is dangerous."

"Just read this," she said, handing me her phone. "Check my text messages. "I'm so embarrassed!" she said, covering her face with her blanket as I read to myself.

Nneka: I've been catching up on my soca, you would be proud

Rishi: Thats good where u say ur parents are frm?

Nneka: They're born here, but my grandparents are Nigerian

Rishi: Right right right . . . yuh ever talk to a Trini bwoy before?

Nneka: No . . .

Rishi: Yuh sure yuh can handle we?

Nneka: Should I be scared?

I paused to look at Nneka. I pulled the blanket from her face. "Nneka, this is totally normal. He's talking about dating! That's good, right?"

"Keep going," she said, covering her face again.

Rishi: Not scared, but u gotta be ready. Yuh think u can keep up wit meh?

Nneka: I can barely keep up with the music . . . Lol

Rishi: Heres my dad's latest mix

Rishi: https://soundcloud.com/DJJumpStart/toronto-summer-vibes-soca-mix

Nneka: Thanks

Rishi: np

Rishi: Hey lemme see you wine to de mix . . .

Nneka: Um . . . I guess next time we hang out?

Rishi: Jus send me a vid

Nneka: Now?!

Rishi: Ya why not

Nneka: I'm a lil shy

Rishi: Why cuz of ur size? Because ur not mawga like your friend?

"Whoa," I said, afraid to continue reading. "This escalated quick."

Nneka: Because I usually don't take videos of myself like that

Rishi: send me a pic then. u playing mas with Liberation right? Send me your pics frm last yrs costume

Nneka: I didn't play mas last year. This will be my first year.

Rishi: Lemme see how u look up close nah? u don't have any pics?

Nneka: What do you mean up close?

Rishi: u kno what i mean. Send me something niceeee. Lemme see yuh shape.

Nneka: Like a selfie?

Rishi: Send me the sexiest pic in yuh phone

Nneka: oh ok . . .

There was a gap in time, after the photo was sent. She looked amazing that day, I could remember. We'd gone to Canada's Wonderland and she wore a cute jean one-piece jumper. In the photo she had an innocent smile and was holding a stuffed animal she won. Not exactly sexy, but very cute.

Maybe Rishi looked at the photo but got busy and couldn't respond. Nevertheless, Nneka continued the conversation a few hours later.

Nneka: Hey Rishi. I'm not sure if you got my last message, but if you're not busy this week maybe we can hang out? Grab some Tims or something casual?

"That's it?" I asked Nneka carefully. She peeked from out of her blanket; her eyes were still damp.

"How humiliating. He ghosted me."

"Let's not jump to conclusions yet . . ." I said, checking the date and time. It hadn't even been a full twenty-four hours yet. "You're only now telling me?"

"I was so embarrassed."

"It's not that bad."

"I know, but I finally got the nerve to ask him out and he

vanished. I'm planning to just avoid him for eternity."

"But he's at the camp every day. How can you avoid him?" I asked, kissing my teeth in frustration. "He could have at least responded. Ugh. Everything seemed cool the other day."

"Exactly," she said, retreating back under her blanket.

"It felt a lil' harsh reading those descriptions of us," I said, rubbing her arm. "Eff him."

"I don't even know why I thought this was a good idea," Nneka said, beginning to cry.

"Just try not to overthink it, okay?"

"Did I say something wrong?" she asked, coming up for air again. She jolted upright and leaned over to grab the small bucket, vomiting another stream of water into it. Tears continued to fall down her face and I was at a loss for words.

"You're still taking all those supplements and teas? And wearing that waist trainer?"

"Yes," she said, looking down sheepishly. "I'm gonna take a shower. Do you mind hanging around for a bit?"

We went out to get some fresh air, and sat at the park in our neighbourhood after Nneka changed. I was still worried, but didn't know if I could handle what was going on by myself.

CHAPTER SIXTEEN
Miss Thicky

I texted Akie and she left the mas camp immediately to come pick us up from the park; we took Nneka to a walk-in clinic for an assessment. The physician was worried after I gave him the rundown. Nneka sat quietly in embarrassment. He pleaded with her to resume her regular eating habits and drink plenty water, then sent her for bloodwork. There was a lab on-site.

"Please, girls. Be very careful about what you see online. Especially if it has to do with your health," he said, with a deep sigh. "My daughter is around your age, so I know you see a lot of products and things online and they're easy to order, but . . . please. When it comes to your health, just ask your family doctor, okay?" he pleaded with us both. He made notes and let Nneka know her doctor would follow up with the bloodwork results.

Nneka confessed everything to Akie during the car ride. She drove quietly and listened, parking up at the far end of the lot before we went inside the mas camp to work for the evening. Nneka didn't want to stay home. It was already after seven and Akie had a lot of work to catch up on.

"You are a brilliant, beautiful young lady," Akie said, after Nneka and I brought her up to speed. "I know you don't want to involve your parents, but you have to promise me that your behaviour will change or I will have to let them know."

"I know, Akie. We didn't want to put you in an awkward position," I told her.

"Is this just about the costumes, Nneka? Is there anything else . . . deeper going on?" Akie asked, carefully. "It's a crazy world out there, so I just want to be sure."

"No, it's really just me panicking and being an idiot," Nneka said, fresh tears falling from her eyes. "I don't feel like myself lately. And the costume is just the starting point. I look in the mirror and I don't love who I see back . . . not like I used to. Especially being around all these yoga girls and models . . . it's a reminder that we're leaving high school and have to compete on a bigger stage. It's scary, to be honest."

"Honey, I hate that this has triggered so much doubt for you," Akie said, taking a deep breath. "You have always been such a beautiful, smart and vibrant soul. Ever since you were younger. All of the external is just extra. You are already perfect just as you are."

"I know, Auntie. I just think this is so exciting but also . . ." Nneka paused. "I feel like 'Bana just put extra pressure on me that I didn't have before."

"Carnival really isn't about that. I know the costumes are . . . scanty at times, but it's really supposed to be a celebration, you know? Coming together on the road, feeling free and dancing like no one's watching . . . even though there are thousands of people watching. In some ways, the exposure and costumes are a part of that freedom . . . being able to share our culture with the world. Proudly. It really isn't about our bodies as much as it is about just being together. Boldly."

"I know," Nneka said. "It all looks so fun and wonderful. And when you see everyone dancing on the street it looks amazing, it's just . . . this." She pointed at her stomach and shuddered.

"No one out there will judge you as harshly as you judge yourself, that's one thing I learned about carnival costumes," Akie began. "But honestly, what was most important to me was having you girls here with me for my first summer back in Toronto. I've gone through a rough couple of years, and I really want to be strong for you. To empower you girls. Life is rough, but it's events and celebrations like this that give us the strength to keep going. That's what I wanted to share . . . but

I don't want to pressure you. If you don't want to participate, that's fine too, honey. I'll understand."

"I know, Auntie. I appreciate what you're doing for us," Nneka said. "I've been learning about the history of carnival and I understand why you love it so much."

"Nneka," I started, lightly tapping my hand on Akie's dashboard, "the costume is a way for us to show our bravery, and have the full 'Bana experience, you know? Plus, Akie is going to make those adjustments for us and add some extra fabrics and feathers here and there, right?"

"Exactly!" said Akie. "That's the spirit. I'll make any necessary adjustments so you're both feeling like yourselves. I'll make sure your costume is comfortable and modest, okay?"

"I know. I want to be there for both of you. And I want to overcome . . . whatever this feeling is. But what about de bwoy Rishi?" Nneka said. "How do I face him in the camp every week, knowing that he dissed me?"

Akie kissed her teeth. "Just brush him off as someone that clearly isn't mature enough to interact with you, even in innocent conversations. You just keep your head up and he'll eventually vanish to you."

"Easier said than done," Nneka said as she watched Rishi hop out of his black Honda coupe wearing a leather backpack and fresh pair of sneakers.

"Keep your head up," Akie said. "You wanted to shoot your shot, and you did. It didn't go as you wanted, but there's nothing to be ashamed of. You still have your dignity, I promise you."

"Thanks, Auntie Akilah."

Rishi was already standing at the back door and taking his mini-bar out of his bag when we exited the car and walked toward the camp door. He watched us approach carefully.

"What's up, Miss Thickas?" Rishi called out to Nneka with an air kiss. I didn't like the hungry look in his eyes. Instant ick. "Miss Thicky! Sexy!" he continued when Nneka didn't respond.

"Her name is Nneka," I said to him curtly, rolling my eyes. I couldn't resist.

"*Miss Thicky*?" Nneka's energy changed and we could both feel it. Her anger returned. Akie stepped ahead before Nneka had a chance to explode.

"Watch yourself, yute," Akie said to him, tapping the brim of his hat. He smiled. "Yuh fadda right there." Akie nodded toward Jump Start's SUV as he was pulling up. "And he won't mind if I cuss yuh. Again."

"Again?" Nneka and I both remarked.

"No manners," Akie continued. "I can't even say he has no broughtupsy, because his parents are good people. He better watch himself."

CHAPTER SEVENTEEN
Drink Water

Each day at the camp was better than the last. We decided to act like Rishi didn't exist, and I let Kyle know that we weren't impressed with his cousin. He tried to apologize on his behalf, explaining that Rishi truly did think Nneka was cute, but it wasn't enough for us. He needed to grow up.

Soon, we became familiar with all the hit soca songs, the lyrics, and learned the Road March from Trinidad's carnival earlier in the year. "You didn't know the songs the other day, and now I hear you singing all the words normal normal," Kyle said to me with a wink when he stopped at our workstation on his way into the camp one afternoon. Rishi knew better and kept his distance. Mainly to avoid Akie's wrath!

"How could I not learn the Road March?" I teased back,

hoping to impress him with my new soca knowledge. He was growing on me — he always knew what memes and videos to send to make me laugh out loud. Day and night.

"Hear you!" he replied, squeezing my shoulder as he walked past. We studied everyone and soon even started to feel some of the basic dance movements — the yoga girls were always dancing and wining up after their sessions. Sometimes we'd watch and learn at the camp and then go home to practice.

With each week, we found ourselves loosening up. We'd chat more with the other teenagers who started to come around, and even stayed later into the night when the liquor seemed to flow and music cranked up. The work always kept its pace.

Nneka did her best to avoid Rishi, and both Akie and I made sure she was eating healthy and staying hydrated. Her doctor said her potassium and sodium levels were low, and she was going to follow up with her weekly and help her find a healthier weight loss plan that included exercise. I promised I'd join her in any activity she wanted.

***

"Good afternoon," Rishi managed to whisper, catching us off guard when Akie left the camp with a couple other women to go to the craft store. "Allyuh good?" he said, trying to sound polite.

"Avoid me, please," Nneka said, turning away.

"Watch yourself," I warned him, not wanting to make a scene. "How you doing, Kyle?" I asked my friend, who stood beside Rishi in support.

"I'm good, but we were wondering if we could take you two out later?" Kyle asked politely, trying to make up for his cousin's antics.

"We're good, thanks," Nneka said to him.

"Yuh look more than good," Rishi said under his breath, slurring. He couldn't resist, followed by a few more mumbled words . . . "round" and "sweet" and others that made Kyle punch him quickly on the arm. He was lucky we didn't understand him.

"I'll link you later," Kyle said apologetically to me, with a shrug.

Rishi didn't give up. He was always staring at Nneka while we were working, and all up in her social media liking and commenting on her posts with hearts or fire emojis or words like "luscious" until she decided to block him. We tried to not let him faze us, and I was relieved when Nneka started talking to Jaheir again — he was making her laugh with his voice notes like the good old days, which was nice to see.

Akie told Nneka that she was out of Rishi's league and sang another soca song as a reminder: "Drink water and mind yuh business!"

CHAPTER EIGHTEEN

Junior Carnival

The band members prepared around the clock for the Junior King and Queen Showcase in mid-July, followed by the Junior Parade. The children's costumes were bright and joyful, and it was a treat to see the babies, toddlers and pre-teens trying on costume pieces and getting measured for their big day. We were more than happy to help with their prep and enjoyed their excited young conversation about the costumes.

We didn't have any duties on Junior Parade day, but Akie brought us out early on the Saturday morning to see the tiny masqueraders arrive with their parents and the Liberation Mas team unload the large children's floats — beautiful constructions built to sit on the frame of the young Junior King and Junior Queen, and be paraded in competition.

I could feel a shift in momentum as we got closer to carnival day. If the early morning of the Junior Parade was that electric, I could only imagine how wild the Grand Parade would be!

"Walking through the crowd is practically dancing!" Nneka exclaimed as we manoeuvred the roads with the team.

"That's the key! You gotta move along with them!" I said, bouncing along to the music and trying to keep up with Akie. "You gotta *chip*!" I used my new carnival vocabulary with her.

We marched along with the dancing Liberation Junior Masqueraders in their little headpieces and sparkly arm bands. Face painters had given each participant a pop of colour to match their costumes and showcase for the judges, while the tiniest of masqueraders — joined by their section leaders, parents and loved ones — marched and danced through the streets of Malvern in Scarborough. They brought music, life, joy and culture to the neighbours watching from their balconies or from lawn chairs by the side of the road. Costumed infants in strollers and proud grannies with sun hats marched along with their families.

The Junior Parade lasted all day until the sun set on the gathering in the park. We found the Liberation station and saw familiar faces from the camp.

"The kiddies looked amazing," I said to Ms. Ingrid when I saw her seated in a lawn chair eating roasted corn on the cob.

"I'm sure we'll win Junior Band of the Year," she said confidently. "I usually have a good feeling about these things. I'm not just saying it because it's us."

"When are the results released?"

"Maybe in the next hour or two. They email us or someone will call to report," she said, looking out proudly at the gathering of families.

Ms. Ingrid was right. Just after Akie dropped us home that evening, the results were in and Liberation's Junior Masqueraders had won. After the kiddie carnival, we began to package and finalize our adult costumes. As the big parade date was approaching, the real countdown began.

Nneka printed labels and coordinated ribbons and decals for the costume boxes. I was responsible for folding and placing the items in the boxes before Akie did the final scan, checking off lists and sealing the boxes for pickup.

We measured and decorated arm bands and helped Akie carefully jewel headpieces. And in the middle of production, we'd still end up two-stepping to old calypso classics and soca hits with our new community.

"What school you guys go to?" one of the newest young men on the scene asked me one evening while I was labelling another complete costume.

"Just graduated from Louis March Secondary," I said,

looking around to see if Kyle was on-site. He wasn't.

"I thought you looked familiar," he continued, rubbing his chin. "You know Tara and Vanessa Santos? The twins?"

"Of course. Those are our girls."

"Okay, Tara said she was gonna play mas with Liberation because her friends worked here," he said. "What's your name?"

"Karla," I told him, holding on to his extended hand. He lingered. "And this is Nneka," I said. She was distracted watching the ladies of Merlot fitting an Ultra Frontline headpiece on one of the models. The colours and details were fascinating. Also fascinating: her breast implants and tiny waist!

"Nice to meet you both," he said as his phone started to ring and he walked away. "Yo, just check the SocaReggaeToronto page to see how much tickets are at the door," he said to his caller, frustrated.

After that, we also found the SocaReggaeToronto TikTok account and made sure to tune in to see videos and clips from the late-night boat rides and related buzz of pre-carnival nightlife. Some of the top soca artists from Trinidad would be in Toronto in the upcoming weeks, and they were posting promotional videos too. We weren't old enough to go to most of the events, but we were definitely old enough to party at the parade and couldn't wait for the day to come!

Our social media window gave us access to the boat rides, clubs, outdoor festivals, all the mas camps and the DJs — the carnival content was overflowing and we loved it! We made sure to take advantage of any opportunity we had at the camp to dance and hang outside. The closer we got to carnival day, the more the party seemed to move to the Liberation headquarters.

We were all happy to see Jamar arrive at the camp. He rushed up behind his mother to place his hands over her eyes. She immediately stood up and tears fell when she embraced her son.

"Surprise!" Jamar said, kissing his mom on the cheek.

"I thought you said your flight came in tomorrow!" she said, not even bothering to wipe her tears. She missed him so much and talked about him every day.

"Wuddup cuz?" I said, extending my arms for a hug. I hadn't seen him in person since before the pandemic. He looked great.

"Heeeey, Karla!" he said, giving me a warm hug. Nneka sat quietly behind me, glue gun in hand, being careful not to drip anything on the fabric. "Miss Nneka! Long time no see!" Jamar said. She placed the jewel carefully on the headpiece before standing up to hug my cousin.

"Hey, Jamar! How's the knees and such?" she teased. We all knew his physio TikTok videos were a hit.

"Well, I've decided to take my content on a road trip and incorporate music and dance into my teachings," he told us.

"Smart move," I said to him, knowing he'd easily find a ton of opportunities to record and share his adventures in Toronto.

Jamar's arms were huge; he had been hitting up the gym and it showed. I could see the curious eyes of the young ladies around the camp looking in our direction at the unfamiliar face, but Jamar was unfazed. He was there to take care of his mother and quickly ordered her some Uber Eats.

"First things first," he said to Akie. "I know you, and I know you probably haven't been eating so don't think you're bringing those bad habits with you to Canada. You need to balance your time, your energy and your nutrition," he scolded lightly. "She does this every year," he told us. "Carnival season comes and her health goes downhill."

I looked at Nneka carefully concentrating on her work.

"Jamar, don't overreact," Akie tried to brush him off.

"Nah, I need you to stay healthy," he said.

When the delivery was close by, Jamar asked Nneka to follow him outside to wait while I continued to hold a wire frame for Akie as she fastened a connection. She had a new glow to her, now that Jamar was there, and I hoped she was taking as good care of her health as Nneka was. There were times I had to force her to eat or she complained of headaches and cramping, but she was making an effort. I didn't realize it then, but Akie was weaker than usual.

They returned with four salads and frozen fruit juices for us. We enjoyed our meals and continued to work until the mas camp got louder and the energy increased with midnight approaching.

"You're in good shape," one of the pretty yoga girls said to Jamar, walking past him with a smile. "Come join me in my demo?" she asked, nodding toward a camera crew setting up in a corner of the camp.

"Excuse me?" Jamar said with a grin, surprised at her introduction.

"My name is Rehana. Would you like to be a part of my demo?" she asked. "For TikTok," she continued. "I'll be posting it tonight. I'm doing a countdown to 'Bana and I'm trying to show that yoga is for everyone."

"I'm not even prepared," he said, looking down at his joggers and t-shirt. "I mean, I guess I'm dressed okay, but I have no idea what I'm doing."

"Da'iz de point," she said with a flirty smile. Jamar shrugged and followed her across the room. I could see a few others watching the new fella as he went over.

CHAPTER NINETEEN

King and Queen

On Thursday and Friday evening the week before the parade, we stayed with Akie to distribute costumes. Even Mom was there to proudly give the masqueraders in our section their goodie bags filled with water bottles, lollipops, lip gloss, sanitizer and extra glitter and gems for their skin on carnival day. Our social media showed Rishi and Kyle helping DJ Jump Start pick up giveaways and party favours for the weekend ahead. Everyone was busy.

"Can I have your attention please," Ms. Ingrid said into the microphone the Wednesday evening before the carnival.

"I just want to thank you all for your hard work this season. On behalf of Gladys and the entire executive team, we are so very proud of our performance already, proud of how the costumes look and are ready to reveal our large pieces tomorrow at King and Queen!"

Everyone cheered and a few banged on tables. The following night, all of the large masquerade bands would be competing for individual large costumes in an extravagant showcase downtown at Lamport Stadium.

***

On Thursday, we worked for an hour before Akie called an Uber to take us to the big show. We excitedly took in the lights of the 401 to the DVP and Gardiner until the driver paused at the end of a congested road and shrugged.

"This is Dufferin and over there is Liberty . . . do you want to wait or just . . . walk?" he asked hesitantly, gesturing at the heavy traffic ahead.

"We'll walk, thanks," Akie said to him, nodding for us to open the side door. "Have a good night . . . and weekend. It's gonna be a busy one!"

"Oh, Caribana weekend is always exciting," he said, grinning. "And I get to see all the costumes up close!"

Akie texted one of the band members, who met us outside Lamport with wristbands to access the venue. We excitedly followed him through the gathering crowd and into the entrance for participants. The soca music echoed throughout the arena and the concrete tunnels as we walked.

Nneka pinched my arm.

"Okay, we're only staying for like an hour and then we have to go back to the camp," Akie said, raising her voice as we neared the end of the hall and walked out of the opening to the field. My eyes widened. Nneka squealed.

On the elevated stage facing the bleachers was an enormous white and silver butterfly with neon accents and blue patterns that sparkled. A leggy sister dressed in silver tights held on to the handles of the construction and firmly walked to the beat of the song, pulling the butterfly with her.

"This is Butterfly Bliss from Jubilee Carnival," the announcer said, lowering the music as he spoke. "In costume, we have Trina Zagar."

Trina worked that costume! She smiled and sang along to the tune while she led the butterfly that stood three times her height across the stage. With bright eyes, she looked out at the crowd cheering her on from the bleachers. She extended her arms to them as she spun. It was fabulous.

It took four men dressed in black Jubilee Carnival t-shirts to help lead Trina and her costume to the side of the stage, down a ramp and around the side of the track where a dozen other constructions waited in line for their time in the spotlight.

It was exciting to see all the floats gathered together in their magnificence. I was still amazed that the carnival judges actually had to select from all these pieces. The competition was fierce!

The next contestant for Queen of the Carnival managed to upstage Trina's elegant butterfly. Instead, black and deep purple glittery peacock feathers made their way up the ramp, with the operator wearing a bright purple catsuit and tall black boots. The contestant had a jeweled purple mask covering her eyes and wore long gloves. She immediately began to spin in wide circles across the stage.

"This is Monica Emanuel for Liberation Mas . . . in Obsidian Nights," the MC said. Akie began to cheer and clap along with the Liberation folks around us at the side of the waiting area. The young lady carrying the costume was so strong, making it move like it was made of feathers.

"Watch this," Akie warned us, winking. Just then, Monica's costume began to bloom neon stems from behind her that lit up into vines. Grape vines with glowing spheres.

Nneka and I both started to clap. It was fantastic! The crowd loved it and the Liberation folks around us shouted loudly and proudly.

"Yes, Monica!" a voice called out.

"That's our Queen!" Ms. Ingrid said, unable to contain her

excitement. If I were to ask her, she'd probably say she had a good feeling about this one.

After Monica did a few broad laps of the stage, the marshals helped her exit and the Liberation team gathered to take apart the large pieces so Monica could step out of the costume.

"She was amazing!" Akie said. "Amazing. Her mom went to school with me and Courtney. She will probably win Queen . . . again."

Our night at the show ended after Monica came off stage. Akie reminded us that the carnival was days away and that we had to return to work. We finished off the packaging for the out-of-town masqueraders and retreated to the back room for cold drinks and fruit. A few others hung around, but the camp was quiet; most people were at the King and Queen showcase.

"Okay . . . it's now the moment of truth," Akie said, reaching into the cabinet beneath the worktable and pulling out two boxes that had our names on the labels.

We were able to go to the changerooms in the back and try on our pieces without an audience.

"I'm not ready!" I squealed, covering my eyes with my hands. The entire season, Akie had been working on our costumes in private.

Pretty and pink, my spandex shorts were snug and my crop

top was covered in gold and teal gems with a halter that tied around my neck. I put on the costume gold neckpiece with a huge teal gem in the center, followed by my jeweled arm sleeves, then tied my leg pieces on.

Next, I rested the feathered wire backpack on my shoulders and smiled at how the pink feathers looked next to my face. The final piece: my gold gemmed tiara headpiece. I squealed in delight.

CHAPTER TWENTY
Emancipation

"Neeks!"

"Karlaaa! Auntie Akilah is a miracle worker!" Nneka called out, loud enough for Akie to hear her and return. Akie came rushing over and clasped her hands together.

"Girls!" she said, raising her eyebrows and pursing her lips. "I think I'm going to cry!" she continued, motioning for us to spin around. "Just beautiful. Gorgeous. Both of you. How does it feel? Comfortable?"

"It's perfect," Nneka said first, staring back at herself in the wall of mirrors across from the change tents. Her costume modification was sleek and still sexy — modest yet funky. The corset hugged her curves and the extra fabric hanging from her jeweled belt was whimsical and pretty. Nneka also had a small backpack of feathers and the same gold tiara as me. We started to dance around to music only we could hear.

Then Nneka started to cry.

"Honey!" Akie said, reaching for her hand.

"This is so beautiful, Auntie. I shouldn't have doubted the costume part . . . I know I've been feeling this way for a while now. About my body. I haven't said anything, but I've been obsessing over it. I'm sorry to drag you two into my mess. Sorry if I'm ruining this experience. This is so pretty," she sobbed. "And comfortable."

"Nneka, don't even apologize! It's a process. And I'm here for you," I said to my friend, wiping away my own tear.

"We are here for you. You heard Jamar, I have to be careful with my health too. We'll learn and grow together, okay? And I'm so glad we get to play ah mas together!" Akie immediately changed the mood.

"This really is beautiful, and so comfortable," I said. I looked at my reflection, admiring the conservative crop top and the extra beading. "I know this took you forever!"

"I wanted you both to feel like yourselves," Akie said, smiling proudly. "And I wanted to surprise you with it. You both feel okay for the road on Saturday?" she asked carefully, looking us each in the eyes. "I listened to you closely all summer and tried to make it something you would feel comfortable with on the GO train, on the street . . . in photos."

"It's comfortable," Nneka said proudly, turning around to look at her rear and drying her eyes. "I'm still lookin' round and rosy . . . but not overly exposed. I can definitely work with this."

We returned to Akie's table to pack up before heading home for the evening. Nneka was sleeping over and we spent the night in our costumes, dancing and bending and preparing ourselves for every possible scenario on the road. We even did a mock restroom stop in my tiny basement bathroom to see how we'd manage with the portable toilets and all those feathers. We checked and re-checked our costumes from every mirror angle possible.

Vanessa: See you on de road!!!!!

Karla: So exciteeeeeddddd

We decided to rest on Friday: hydrate and get ready for the long day on the parade route. Nneka and I ate lots of fruits, drank lots of water and did a lot of stretching. We combed every inch of TikTok and Instagram to see what Liberation Mas and the other bands had posted from the competition the night before. We looked at other groups of friends showcasing costume pieces and pre-carnival preparations and couldn't help but get anxious with each post.

Tara: I'm too excited to sleep

Karla: Literally me!

The music alone had us in good spirits. We photographed every detail of our costumes and sent them to the twins, who were also at home listening to soca and packing their camera equipment.

"You two ready for de road?" my dad asked us, peeking into my opened bedroom door.

"So ready!" I exclaimed, still wearing my headpiece. We were trying out some of Nneka's bright eyeshadows and glitters under my ring light to see what would look best in the sun.

"Ekene and Jamar are troopers. I hear they're going to take you downtown?" Dad said, looking at the costume pieces across my bed. I knew they were modest enough, because he nodded slowly in approval at the shorts and tank.

"Yes, Mr. Hall, Ekene will drive us and bring us home. Jamar said he'll go down with Auntie Akilah, but they'll both be with us all day," Nneka clarified.

"I feel much better knowing that," he said. "When I was

younger, back when the parade was on University Avenue, it was a different vibe. You had real live bands playing. Still really crowded, but it was different. I haven't been back since I was a yute."

"Oh, trust me, Daddy, I've seen older women picking up costumes. Like, older than you and Mom. They still out there having fun!"

"For real?" Dad said, smiling. "You know I don't have the patience for those crowds. I love my people, but you will not catch me downtown in that chaos!" He laughed. "I'll just watch the news and hope to catch a glimpse of those costumes you've been working on!"

CHAPTER TWENTY-ONE

Bacchanal Time

Ekene looked awesome! When he came to pick me up, he was dressed in teal from head to toe — teal shorts and tank top, armbands, leg bands, even the glitter smeared on his skin. He took off his shades as he approached the door.

"Mr. and Mrs. Hall, I promise to keep an eye on these girls downtown and bring Karla home safely to you this evening," he said, greeting my parents at the door.

"We appreciate you," Mom said, taking a quick pic of him with her phone. She had been taking pictures of me all morning with a proud smile. "It almost feels like a rite of passage. My baby's first carnival . . . as a costume maker!"

"Mom," I said, laughing.

"I know. Just have fun and stay close together. I know

Akilah will be around, but just look out for each other, okay?"

"Yes, Mommy," I said, kissing her, intentionally leaving glitter on her from my cheek.

"Okay, no dancing for television cameras," Dad continued to recite a list of rules for me as I slid on my new pink and comfortably flat carnival-friendly boots. "Try to stay away from really thick parts of the crowd, or if you see people breaking fences or unnecessary trouble . . . just go the other way. Stick close to your band and the trucks. Drink lots of water."

"Oh-em-gee! Yes, Daddy!" I said, rolling my eyes at him. "You sound like Dorian! He texted me a long list of rules last night."

"Because Dorian used to be one of those young men out there on the streets . . . he knows how wild it can get!"

"Aw, Nneka! Look at you!" Mom let the tears fall this time. "Beautiful. Just beautiful," she said. "You are so good at makeup."

"Thank you, Mrs. Hall," she said, kissing Mom's other cheek, deliberately leaving a mark of bright lipstick.

In just a few hours, we entered a new reality downtown! After walking through the grounds to find the meeting location for Liberation, our band started its journey through the parade route. We walked along with the other hundred masqueraders in our section in a large colour-coordinated lineup.

Moving through the sea of revellers felt like walking through some fantasy land where everything sparkled, everyone was happy, all things were beautiful and the only thing you were expected to do was have fun. And dance!

Each step deeper into the crowds, I could feel just how special this tradition was. I could see it on everyone's face: it was their favourite time of year.

Our band started on the CNE grounds and went through paths and roads together, making the journey toward Lakeshore Boulevard.

"Liberation Mas! Stay in yuh section! Stay in yuh section!" Jump Start chanted into the microphone while an instrumental of a soca song played. "All yuh lookin' good out there! Just stay in yuh section!"

The sound of his voice gave the masqueraders some energy; the walking turned into strutting, and the dancing picked up. Nneka and I had been practicing all summer: we were ready to go! With water bottles in hand, we smiled; the music sounded so good we couldn't help ourselves but jam!

An older teen boy watched Nneka dance for a few minutes before rubbing his hand on her bare shoulder. Glitter and all.

"What the?" I heard Nneka say, looking at me with wide eyes. He kept going.

He was just her type: fair brown skin, big curly hair and

a bright smile. He pulled her into a hug. "Pretty in that pink."

"I don't know you like that, bruh," Nneka responded politely. My girl had been on point all day, keeping her personal space and telling the boys to keep their hands to themselves. She pointed her bright pink nails with an extended wrist, indicating that we should rejoin Akilah near the truck. He shrugged and continued to move through the crowd, reaching out to hug another girl in our section with the same line.

"Hey!" Akie called out from the side of the truck where she sat, wearing her own tall pink boots and drinking from a plastic pink cup. We waved back up to her.

Ekene danced with any and every girl around us, smiling and making everyone feel comfortable by asking their approval first. Somehow it felt like we were being approached first and asked questions afterward.

"Wha gwaaan?" another guy said, squeezing in between Nneka and I near the truck. He was wearing our costume and pieces we had personally constructed. That alone brought us joy, taking in his headpiece and the careful beading we had done.

"What's your name?" he asked Nneka politely with a wide grin. His friend walked shyly behind us. "I'm Evan."

"My name is Nneka," I heard her say to him over the pounding music. The DJ shouted above the song, asking everyone to wave their flags as we continued down the road. A Bahamian flag flew across my forehead.

"Ah, a Nigerian name." I continued to listen, watching Nneka carefully to make sure she felt okay. Earlier, her weary eyes had me worried.

"You're Nigerian?" Nneka's eyes lit up.

"Nah, my parents are Jamaican, but I have nuff Nigerian bredrens. Two of them have sisters named Nneka," he said, smiling. "You live here in Toronto?"

"Ya. Well, Scarborough," she said to him.

"Okay, okay. I'm in Markham," he continued, pulling out his phone from a neon yellow satchel strapped across his chest. "Yo, can I get your Snap? I've been watching you dance, but I know we might end up getting separated in the crowd."

"Um, okay. Sure," Nneka said, pulling out her phone and opening the app. I looked around to see if Ekene was paying attention, but he was busy dancing with two older women, one on each arm. Living his best life, with Jamar taking video of him from his spot on the truck next to Akie.

Akie was exhausted and had been up on the truck for most of the day. I had a feeling she hadn't slept. She still looked cute in her shades, her hair coated in a fresh pink dye to match our costumes. She swayed slightly to the music, sipping a drink as she danced. Akie would always be cool, confident and sexy at any size, in any location. I knew that for a fact. Even when she was half-asleep.

Sure enough, the truck sped up and we were separated from the boys, so we continued to follow at our own pace. It was easy to stay together because we always had Akie in our sight. As long as we were close to her, we would be close to each other.

The crowd swept us into a frenzy as one of the summer's hit soca songs played again — it had been playing all day. Nneka and I continued to dance and walk, sipping our water and letting the sun shine on us, embraced by the thumping bass and the breeze with feathers blowing around us and rhythmic energy coming from every direction.

"Best day ever!" Vanessa screamed out, returning to chip with us. She and Tara had been busy trying to capture every side of the parade so far. They went from the truck to the road and even the sidelines to film the masqueraders in action.

"I know!" I agreed, smiling and waving into Tara's camera before they continued in the opposite direction of the crowd, letting the dancers pass and pose with Vanessa.

There were so many people pushing, dancing and passing by that I didn't realize someone was trying to dance with me as we moved down the street. He was very tall, with a big messy Afro and a baby face. He was in street clothes but still chose to parade with the costumed masqueraders — intruders to the parade were called "stormers," I learned from Akie, because they were "storming" the parade route.

There were so many stormers, I almost couldn't blame them for wanting to join in the fun and dance with us. As long as they kept it respectful, we didn't mind. It was hard to keep track with the crowd moving and the music guiding us all. When I paused to look at the face of the boy dancing behind Nneka, I was surprised to see a tipsy Rishi with his hands waving in the air, marching behind my good sis. Kyle and their friends were close behind. Kyle gave me a quick side hug before two girls from our band sandwiched him into a quick dance, giggling and blowing their Liberation Mas whistles.

"Thickas! Miss Thicky! Yuh have sugar waist for real!" Rishi called out, staring down at Nneka as she grooved. One thing about my girl, she could move! I saw him reach down and try to grab her behind beneath the extra coverings and fabrics, but there was so much going on she couldn't tell what was happening or where it was coming from.

I reached out to push his hand away from her, but Rishi was unfazed. Kyle had been carried off by the girls and tried to get back to us while I widened my eyes to get Nneka's attention. She looked back and tried to keep cool, rolling her eyes when she saw how sloppy he looked.

"Do not touch me," she said sternly, turning to face him. Kyle looked at me and shrugged in frustration — he had probably been babysitting Rishi all morning.

I motioned for Kyle to take Rishi away, but he shrugged again, shaking his head. "I tried!" he said. "I've been trying all day, trust me." The other boys around him seemed drunk too. "I have about three sets of car keys right now," he said, nodding down to his bag.

"Why yuh treatin' me so bad?" Rishi slurred, leaning into Nneka. "Yuh know I check fi yuh."

"Ease up!" Nneka said forcefully, linking her arm through mine to pull away from Rishi's attempted grip. The crowd made it difficult for us to get away.

"Why yuh so shy? All summer yuh only watchin' watchin'. Lehwe talk nuh?" Rishi continued.

"Bruh. No." Nneka shrugged him off her back, and we pushed into an opening in the crowd until he was out of reach. We kept chipping down the road and stepping away from them, but the boys stayed close behind. Every now and then I felt a body dancing behind me, though everything moved so quickly I barely had time to check who was who!

Jamar caught my eye and gave me a thumbs up with raised eyebrows from the truck. He gestured to the crowd to see if I needed help. I shook my head, grateful that his eyes were there to protect us. His calmness made me feel like I didn't have anything to worry about. It was probably normal carnival behaviour if he didn't feel the need to jump down and save us.

Rishi and his boys got pushed to the other side of the road in the crowd.

"Nneka! Karla!" our friend Emma from elementary school called out, giving us quick hugs as we danced. "I haven't seen you two in so long!"

"Ah!" I squealed, hugging our old neighbour. "You still in Brampton?"

"Yeah, but I'm going to TMU in the fall. Where are you guys going?" she said loudly, over the sound of DJ Jump Start's instructions.

"*Wave! Wave!*" he continued to yell out, and an older man in front of the truck waved a gigantic Liberation Mas flag around his head. The truck driver blew his horn to alert him not to get too close. One of the marshals in a blue Liberation t-shirt carefully protected the flag man from the truck's path. He continued to wave the flag.

"TMU too!" I said. We hugged again quickly and smiled. "See you there!" She was moved away as her friends rejoined her, dancing together in a chain, holding on to one another's shoulders for support as they pushed through the masqueraders.

"Come wine wit me, nah?" Rishi was back, stumbling in our direction with his friends.

"No means no," Nneka sang out to him. She held up her hands so his friends would get the signal. "Come on, guys. Enough!"

"He's so annoying," I said, relinking my arm with Nneka. I wouldn't have minded a quick dance with Kyle, but the rest of their troupe was getting obnoxious too. The street continued to get more congested in the afternoon and we could feel the crowd's momentum picking up. We managed to get a snack from the band and refill our water bottles. We even found someone handing out popsicles — great under the hot midday sun.

"You okay?" I asked Nneka, taking a moment to look at my bestie.

"I'm okay," she said, with a nod.

"Your stomach?"

"It's fine."

"Any headache?" I asked, knowing her symptoms were still coming and going.

"No headache."

"Okay. Ready for de road?" I threw my popsicle stick into the garbage nearest us, and she did the same.

"Lehwego!"

The next time Rishi and the boys caught up to us, it wasn't so easy to bounce away.

The Liberation truck stopped moving temporarily and the crowd was piling up, looking up at Jump Start while the marshals tried to clear the way to continue.

"Liberation Mas! How yuh feeling?" Jump Start called out, followed by a wave of cheers and whistles blowing.

Kyle could barely keep Rishi standing upright. Rishi started to dance behind Nneka, stuck in the crowd, and reached to wrap his arms around her waist, linking his fingers around her stomach. I could feel Nneka cringe. One of the large gems on her belt fell off.

"Come, nah," Rishi slurred, speaking too close to her face. "I wanna take you on date, Miss Thicky. Sweet and round."

"Ugh!" she warned him, shrugging to release his grip. "Fix up. This isn't cool!" Kyle stared at us apologetically. His friends continued to drink and dance in their own zone.

Nneka was vexed. She looked down at her damaged costume and narrowed her eyes.

"Get lost." I peeled one of Rishi's hands from around Nneka, and he laughed.

"Come on, nah. Is 'Bana time! Why you two acting so stush?" he asked, stumbling back slightly when Nneka elbowed him to make space.

"'Low them," Kyle said, taking Rishi's arm forcefully and attempting to drag him toward the truck now that they were finally close enough. "You know your dad won't let us into any of the fetes this weekend if he's mad at you." Jump Start was now facing our direction with the mic in his hand.

"Watch yuhself, bai!" he said directly to Rishi, nodding at the friends to come his way. "*Liberation Mas have a con-tract*," he sang along to the song playing, never missing a beat. "Bring Rishi come." He looked down at his son in disappointment.

I stepped aside to let Kyle continue to drag Rishi. The other drunken homeboys managed to help lift him up on the truck next to his dad, who had been playing high energy soca hits since we'd left the CNE grounds. We saw him tap Rishi on the back of the head with the microphone and motion for him to sit down.

"What the eff?" I said to Nneka, shaking my head. "Your costume good?"

"Yeah," Nneka said, looking down sadly at the missing jewel. "Ugh."

"I'm sorry," I said, thankful the boys had moved on now that Rishi wasn't stumbling amongst them. Up on the truck, Rishi's dad and Kyle sat him down and he immediately rested his head. He was out. "You okay?"

"I'm okay," Nneka said, shaking her shoulders to snap out of the little funk Rishi had dragged us into.

It was chaos, but we kept moving. Another surge of the crowd nudged us slightly away from the truck and closer to the gated viewing area where a few masqueraders from the other sections were dancing together in their various colours.

We continued on — Liberation Mas embraced us like old friends. DJ Jump Start's voice rang out as he kept up with the pace of the music. "Liberation Mas! Allyuh having a good time? Yuh lookin' good on de Lakeshore today! We ready to take Band of the Year!" The song started over again from the beginning, likely the hundredth time that day.

We raised our hands and continued to walk and dance as though it was the first time we had heard it.

"*Iz we day, iz we day, iz we day*!" we both sang out, following the speakers down the street. Akie pointed over at us, waving in our direction, comfortable on her throne keeping watch.

CHAPTER TWENTY-TWO

Carnival Contract

"I'm cooked!" I said when we collapsed into the back seat of Ekene's car later that afternoon after taking the long, obstacle course walk back up Lakeshore through the crowds, across the CNE grounds and further down the road to the parking lot.

We were all happy to remove our headpieces; Ekene turned up the air conditioner and continued to remove his arm and leg bands, then took off his sneakers and slid into a pair of Crocs he had on standby.

Beyond exhausted, we were grateful for the seat.

"Yo! Meh get nuff gyal today!" Ekene said, laughing. He was a handsome fella with a nice smile and always full of charm. "Jamar is jokes! I'm glad he had fun. I can't wait to see what content he puts out on his channel. He was out there all day talking about girls with *good knees* and breaking it down in medical terms."

"You guys make a good team! You were like his wing man," I said, laughing. "I saw you two in action. I had so much fun, I couldn't even stand it."

Nneka and I had lots to talk about but stayed quiet with Ekene within earshot. He was going to drop us home and take a quick nap before getting ready for a soca concert with Jamar and his friends that evening at an outdoor park. We would have loved to tag along but knew our parents wouldn't go for it as long as we were underage. I was tired, but given the choice I'd find an outfit and be ready to hit the road again!

I couldn't wait to have a video call with Nneka once I was home, showered and refreshed. My parents ordered pizza and wings for dinner and left a plate for me. I recapped the day's events with them in the kitchen as they continued their regular Saturday evening routine — chilling — and I headed to my laptop to chat with Nneka.

"What the entire eff?" she said, opening her eyes wide. She was already in her pajamas and bonnet though it was barely after seven. "Today's giving . . . it's giving . . . monumental. It's giving . . . Cinderella."

"Where do we begin?" I asked her.

"I swear."

"The dancing! The wining! Girl!"

"I felt like . . . I felt confident!"

"Me too! Being outside like that and seeing everyone on the sidelines cheering us on and taking photos . . . so much fun!"

"Crossing the stage was my favourite part. The way they held us back and then let us loose . . . and then everyone, like, wining for their lives! Did you see Akie? She stole the show with that headpiece. The judges loved her. Do you think Liberation Mas will win Band of the Year?"

"I hope so! All of the other costumes and floats looked so good, like, everything was amazing," I said. "I never imagined something could be so incredibly fun."

"Same," Nneka said, looking back to ensure her room door was closed and lowering her voice. "I hate hate hate that Rishi turned out to be such a weirdo, though. He was so unruly!"

"Wild," I agreed, wide-eyed. "Fully weird . . . hopefully one of his friends was recording that."

"Oh, they were," Nneka said. "Did you see Ms. Ingrid? She wasn't impressed."

"She was vex, yo!" I said, laughing. "And don't think Akie didn't see either. She peeped the whole thing."

"He's full of red flags," she said, sighing in disappointment. "He had the whole summer to come correct, and this is how he's going out? Legit wasteman. And he ruined my costume."

"He probably messed up Kyle's whole day too."

"Until his dad put him in the corner! Ha!"

"For real!" I told her, playing the song we'd been hearing all day. "Every time I hear this rhythm, I'll remember this day. This one and the other one about 'carnival in your DNA'!"

"Yes! My new favourite song!" Nneka agreed. "Thanks for encouraging me, girl. I would have hated to miss this . . . everyone had so much fun."

"You feel okay?"

"I do. Well, I'm extremely tired but otherwise okay."

"Okay, good. Vanessa just messaged me."

"I can't wait to see their videos. Everyone looked so good."

"Auntie Akilah was right . . . once you're out there, you don't even feel a way. It was very comfortable and everyone was so welcoming. Like old friends. No wonder Akie travels to all these carnivals. It was a vibe," I concluded.

"That boy we met by the jerk chicken stand has been texting me!" Nneka said, smiling. "He lives in Pickering."

"Sweet," I said to her, checking my phone. There was a string of messages from Kyle. He was venting about Rishi and how Jump Start refused to let them into his party that night — or his boat ride on holiday Monday. Rishi's dad officially put him on punishment, and Kyle as his cousin and number-one sidekick felt like he had to stay behind with him. "Okay, go text the guy back and then get some rest. I'm gonna get the tea from Kyle."

A text had come in from Vanessa while I was chatting with Nneka.

Vanessa: Today was so much funnnnnnnnnnn! I'm so glad we got to hang with you guys at the parade.

Karla: I could do this every summer, I swear.

Vanessa: Me too. Tara says thank you, and to thank your Aunt for letting us record up on the truck. She is beyond fabulous.

Karla: I will.

"Karla! Come look! Akilah's on TV!" Mom called up the stairs to me. I rushed down quickly to catch the end of an interview Akie was giving with a local station.

"Carnival is all about feeling free and being *emancipated*!" She smiled, turning around to showcase her costume. One arm was extended dramatically in the air, modelling the beautiful jeweled sleeve. "My name is Akilah Johnson and this is my Rosé Rendezvous piece that I designed for Liberation Mas! I made sure that everyone who purchased a costume from us felt comfortable to express themselves and their culture today, as you'll see with the various styles."

"This is always one of the best celebrations in the city, attracting participants of all cultural backgrounds and ages," the reporter said, dancing alongside Akie, moving with her flow so she could keep the microphone near. "This was one of my favourite costumes this morning! I was watching you lead your group across the stage with such great moves, and I said . . . this is stunning. The pink, the gold tiara . . . gorgeous."

"This is what carnival is all about! The beauty . . . and a little bit of bacchanal! Feeling good, feeling free and the vibes cyan done!" Akie said, giving the camera a cute Caribbean-style twerk with a smile. A few of the shirtless men in her design and full headpieces joined her and started to vogue around her to the music. "Whether you're in costume or watching from home, the spirit of carnival is all about joy and love and freedom, and it's an honour for me to help create these positive vibes and share this part of our culture."

"Rosé Rendezvous represent! Big up Akilah! *Raaaaay!*" one of the men said mischievously into the microphone, before dancing off.

"Thank you. Akilah Johnson from Liberation Mas, don't let me keep you. Enjoy the rest of the parade!"

Akie continued to smile and dance, then waved at the camera: "Happy Emancipation Month!" she screamed, shaking her shoulders and wining in a quick circle for the viewers. Mom hollered out loud, slapping the table before her in glee at her sister's natural energy. Dad shook his head with a smile, knowing that I had now been officially introduced to this energetic and creative side of our Caribbean culture.

I was just happy to be there.

AUTHOR'S NOTE

Toronto Caribbean Carnival and Caribana

Founded in 1967 as a centennial gift to Canada from the Caribbean Canadian community, the festival originally known as Caribana was created to showcase Caribbean music, dance and masquerade. Today, the parade continues as the Toronto Caribbean Carnival, though many still affectionately refer to it as Caribana or 'Bana, keeping its original spirit alive. The Caribana Arts Group also remains active, hosting Caribana-branded events and cultural initiatives promoting Caribbean art forms rooted in community empowerment.

CARIBBEAN AND CARNIVAL GLOSSARY

backline — the more affordable costume option in a carnival section with a simpler design

band — a group of masqueraders organized under one name and theme, parading together during Carnival

band leader — the person responsible for organizing and managing a carnival band, including its theme, costumes and logistics

broughtupsy — Caribbean slang referring to good manners and respectful upbringing

chip — a relaxed style of dancing or marching to music while moving along the parade route

cyan — Caribbean-English slang for "can't" (e.g., "I cyan believe it!")

fete — a lively Caribbean party, especially one held in celebration of Carnival

frontline — the premium costume option in a carnival section, with a larger, more detailed (and usually more expensive) design

low them — Caribbean expression meaning "leave them alone" or "let them be"

mas camp — the creative hub where costumes are designed, built and distributed leading up to Carnival

mas or **masquerade** — the act of wearing costumes and participating in the Carnival parade

masquerader — a person dressed in costume participating in the Carnival parade

mawga — Caribbean slang for someone who is very skinny or underweight

midline — a costume option that falls between frontline and backline in flair and pricing

play mas or **play ah mas** — to participate in Carnival in costume, dancing on the road

section — a themed subgroup within a band, each with its own costume design

section leader — the individual responsible for managing a specific costume section within a band

stush — Caribbean slang for someone who acts overly proper, snobby or standoffish

ACKNOWLEDGEMENTS

Thank you to Jim Lorimer, Susan Adlam, and the entire Lorimer team for their commitment to amplifying Caribbean Canadian voices in libraries and schools. Additional thanks to Allister Thompson for his insightful guidance and editorial leadership. Sincere appreciation to the Toronto Revellers Cultural Association for the opportunity to learn about carnival firsthand and explore the production and presentation processes of mas in support of this beautiful and liberating celebration.